THE MISSING PASSENGER

THE MISSING PASSENGER

LIARS BOOK 2

Jack Heath

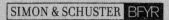

SIMON & SCHUSTER BFYR

NEW YORK LONDON TORONTO SYDNEY NEW DELHI

SIMON & SCHUSTER BFYR

An imprint of Simon & Schuster Children's Publishing Division
1230 Avenue of the Americas, New York, New York 10020

Text © 2018 by Jack Heath
Jacket image texture by nonton/iStock; jacket design
by Greg Stadnyk © 2021 by Simon & Schuster, Inc.,
Originally published in Australia in 2018 by Scholastic Australia as *No Survivors*.
This edition published under license from Scholastic Australia Pty Limited.
First US edition February 2021

SIMON & SCHUSTER BFYR is a trademark of Simon & Schuster, Inc.
For information about special discounts for bulk purchases, please contact Simon & Schuster Special Sales at 1-866-506-1949 or business@simonandschuster.com.
The Simon & Schuster Speakers Bureau can bring authors to your live event. For more information or to book an event, contact the Simon & Schuster Speakers Bureau at 1-866-248-3049 or visit our website at www.simonspeakers.com.
Interior design by Hilary Zarycky
The text for this book was set in New Caledonia.
Manufactured in the United States of America
2 4 6 8 10 9 7 5 3 1
Library of Congress Cataloging-in-Publication Data
Names: Heath, Jack, 1986– author.
Title: The missing passenger / Jack Heath.
Description: First US edition | New York : Simon & Schuster Books for Young Readers, 2021. | Series: Liars ; book 2 | Originally published in Australia in 2018 by Scholastic Australia. | Audience: Ages 12 up. | Audience: Grades 7-9. | Summary: "When a seemingly unoccupied plane crash-lands in the middle of Kelton, Jarli's attempts to lay low and out of Viper's criminal crosshairs crash-lands along with it. The cause of the accident is a mystery until his Truth App uncovers a dangerous secret at the crash site—a secret Viper will do anything to keep buried"—Provided by publisher.
Identifiers: LCCN 2020030135 | ISBN 9781534449893 (hardcover) | ISBN 9781534449916 (eBook)
Subjects: CYAC: Application software—Fiction. | Honesty—Fiction. | Criminals—Fiction.
Classification: LCC PZ7.H3478 Mi 2021 | DDC [Fic]—dc23
LC record available at https://lccn.loc.gov/2020030135

PART ONE
PLANE CRASH

In the speech-to-text code, the phrase *I don't remember* lowers the probability of a lie. Liars rarely admit to forgetting something. They think it's a hole in their story.

−*Documentation from* Truth, *version 2.1*

Ground Zero

Watch out!" Bess yelled.

Jarli looked up from his chips just in time to see the plane screaming toward them. Sunlight bounced off the wings, dazzling him. The stink of jet fuel filled his nose. His eyes widened as he saw the emergency exit gaping open above the whirling engines.

A blast of air hit Jarli like a hurricane, sending him staggering sideways off the footpath. The wind ripped the bag of chips from his hands.

The wings cast triangular shadows, which swept across Jarli and Bess as the plane hurtled over their heads, dropping toward the street.

Jarli couldn't believe it. "They're trying an emergency landing!"

"That's crazy," Bess said. "They'll hit someone's house!"

The left wingtip clipped a streetlight, smashing the top off it. A blizzard of glass rained down. The right wing hit a power pole with a deafening *CLANG*, knocking it flat and snapping the cables. Lights went dead in all the surrounding houses.

"Get down!" Jarli cried. He and Bess hit the ground as a broken power cable whipped through the air above them, shooting sparks. Bess was shouting something, but the engines were too loud. Jarli couldn't hear the words.

When he looked back at the plane, he saw that the landing gear still hadn't come out. With a screech, the belly of the plane hit the street, flinging aluminum splinters in all directions. The wings smashed through hedges, destroying letterboxes and sending wheelie bins flying. One wing hit a parked car, flipping it over and over like in a demolition derby.

Then the plane plowed into the big two-story house at the end of the street. The building *exploded* into a cloud of broken bricks and shattered glass.

Jarli stared in horror, his hands over his mouth. Debris rained down. Dogs were barking all over the neighborhood. The trees, which had been crowded with birds a minute ago, were empty.

"Crikey," Bess whispered. "You think anyone was in there?"

"I sure hope not," Jarli said. He couldn't hear any screaming, but his ears were still ringing.

The hull of the plane had cracked like an egg, spilling jet fuel across the road. Smoke poured from the engines. People would see the black cloud from kilometers away.

Thirty seconds ago the world had seemed so normal. He and Bess had just rented *Snake Man 3* from the old video store on the way home from school. Bess had insisted on walking, despite her crutches. They'd bought hot chips and had been eating them as they strolled back to Jarli's place in the afternoon sun.

Now the sky was black, and the street was strewn with rubble. It was like they had been teleported into a war zone.

Jarli couldn't just stand there. "Are you hurt?" he asked Bess.

Bess had grabbed her crutches and was trying to get up. "No. You okay?"

"Yeah." He helped her to her feet. "Stay back. Call 911."

"What about you? Jarli!"

Jarli was already sprinting toward the downed plane and the smashed house. Someone could be in there, bleeding to death. There was no time to lose.

The closer Jarli got, the worse the smoke became. The turbines in the engines were still spinning, creating a cyclone of unbreathable hot air that baked the insides of his lungs.

"Hello?" Jarli's voice was already raspy from the smoke. "Is anyone in there?"

If anyone replied, he couldn't hear them over the noise of the engines.

The plane lay inside the wreckage of the house. Jarli ran up the driveway and through the smashed front wall until he reached the wing. Broken glass crunched under his shoes. His head was just below the row of passenger windows.

He was afraid of what he might see inside. But he had to

look. Dread filling his stomach, he climbed onto a pile of rubble and peered through one of the smashed windows.

He saw nothing but empty seats.

The plane seemed deserted.

Relieved but wanting to be certain, Jarli circled around to the emergency exit and poked his head in. The plane had room for about a dozen people, but no one was there. Not even the pilot. The cockpit door hung open, revealing shattered controls and an empty seat.

Everyone must have bailed midflight. But why?

Whumpf. Flames raced across a puddle of jet fuel behind him. Jarli jumped away from the intense heat.

If anyone was in the house, he didn't have long to find them. He'd seen how fast a fire like this could spread.

Covering his face with one arm, Jarli stumbled into the wrecked building. Only one wall still stood. The rest looked like ruins from ancient Rome. Chunks of the ceiling were all over the floor. Someone could be underneath the debris. Unconscious, maybe.

Jarli's eyes stung. The puddles of burning fuel were spreading. Behind him, near the remains of the front wall, smashed wooden beams were catching fire. Having barely escaped from a burning warehouse a few months ago, Jarli knew he was running out of time to leave. Soon his lungs would fill with deadly smoke.

But what if someone was still alive in here?

"Hello?" he bellowed and immediately started coughing. There was no response.

Jarli clambered over some rubble, searching for survivors. He lifted a few chunks of brickwork—looking for an arm, a foot, anything. The hot bricks stung his hands. There was nothing underneath them except broken glass.

He passed a smashed TV, then a crumpled fridge. There was a blackened plastic box nearby that might have been a data projector.

Jarli looked back. His heart clenched as he saw that the fire was already climbing the walls. Smoke hid the ceiling, growing thicker every second. Jarli quickened his pace, wading through cutlery and smashed plates. The gas stove was a twisted wreck, lying on its side. This must have been the kitchen.

The back wall of the house was missing, pushed out by the plane. He could see the backyard through the haze. The innards of the house had been scattered across the grass. A queen-size mattress was impaled on the back fence. A chest of drawers floated in the swimming pool—

Wait. Back up. Gas stove.

This house was connected to the gas main. When the flames reached it, the main could explode. Jarli was standing on a time bomb.

The backyard pool was still full of water. It might protect him, but he couldn't just jump in—he had to warn Bess about the gas. He turned and ran back the way he'd come. The fumes from the burning jet fuel still scorched his throat. The smoke surrounded him. He was dizzy and could barely see. The only light came from the flames, blazing all over the shattered beams.

Jarli tripped over a TV and hit the ground. Broken glass stung his palms. He'd already gone past the TV . . . hadn't he? Was he stumbling around in circles? Which way was the front of the house?

Jarli got to his feet and staggered through the smoke in what he hoped was the right direction. The heat stung his eyes, so he closed them. A few steps later, he bumped into a wall.

Only one internal wall had been left standing. At least now he knew where in the house he was. He felt his way across the bricks, eyes stinging.

Then he tripped again and fell.

He hit the floor shoulder first. He tried to get up, but it was hard to figure out which way up was. As he crawled along the hot wood, his arms kept collapsing under him. His muscles felt frail. He couldn't see or breathe. The sound of the roaring flames started to fade. The heat, the light, the smell—everything was slipping out of reach.

"Help me!" A whisper was all he could manage.

Darkness crawled in from the edges of his vision.

False Identity

Strong hands lifted Jarli into the air.

He was at a Paint Rocket concert, crowd-surfing through the noisy darkness. Except he'd never been to a concert. Bands never came to Kelton.

Soon the smoke cleared, or maybe his eyes were just working better. Something huge and yellow filled his vision. When he shifted his head, he realized it was a coat. He could see rivers of grit and ash in the creases of the plastic. He was being carried over the shoulder of a firefighter.

Jarli's ears had recovered just enough for him to hear shouting. Other firefighters were yelling commands at one another. Bess was calling out his name.

It all came back to him. The plane crash. The burning house.

The stove.

"Gas," Jarli mumbled. "Explosion." No one seemed to hear him. The words didn't come out properly. His lips felt stiff, like clay.

When they were a safe distance from the burning plane,

the firefighter set Jarli down on the curb and knelt in front of him. The air seemed impossibly cold. Jarli's teeth were chattering.

"Is anybody else in the house?" the firefighter asked. His gray eyes matched his bristly mustache. His skin was wrinkly except for spots where old burns had made it smooth. His name was stitched onto his uniform—KING.

"Couldn't find anyone," Jarli rasped. "But—"

"No one was in there with you?"

Bess limped over on her crutches. "He wasn't in the house when the plane hit," she told the firefighter. "He ran in to look for survivors. He's like that."

Jarli couldn't tell if she was complimenting him or calling him an idiot. Maybe both. He coughed up a glob of black, shiny spit onto the road. "Gas stove," he gasped. "In the house."

The firefighter was looking at someone over Bess's shoulder. "Hey!" he yelled. "Stay back! Get that kid back!"

Jarli looked. A few meters away, a teenage boy was sprinting toward the burning ruins of the house. He'd dropped his shopping bags, spilling apples and milk onto the road. His face was as white as the plane had been before the fire charred it.

"Mum!" he screamed. "Dad!"

Jarli felt sick. Were the boy's parents in the burning ruins of the house? Had Jarli missed them somehow?

One of the other firefighters grabbed the teenager before

he could get too close to the fire. "You can't go in there," she yelled. "It's too dangerous."

Jarli's eyes were full of soot, sweat, and tears. He blinked, clearing his vision. Now he recognized the woman—her name was Fiona. She worked at the post office with Mum. Jarli hadn't known she was a volunteer firefighter.

He recognized the boy, too. It was Doug Hennessey.

Jarli didn't like Doug. He was a quiet, angry kid who had moved to Kelton last year and spent most of his time in class glaring at people. After Jarli's lie detector app, *Truth*, had gone viral, Doug had cornered Jarli and threatened him.

That didn't mean Jarli was happy to see Doug's home destroyed, though.

"Mum!" Doug wailed again.

"We've searched the house," Fiona said. "There was no one inside."

"Are you sure?" Doug asked. It was strange for Jarli to see someone as scary as Doug look so frightened and desperate.

"We're sure. What's your name?"

Doug just stared at the burning plane and the shattered house.

"Tell me your name," Fiona said. "I'll track down your parents and make sure they're okay."

"Doug Hennessey," Doug said finally.

Jarli's phone beeped in his pocket. *Lie.*

Jarli's jaw dropped. His homemade *Truth* app could detect

lies with 99.2 percent accuracy—using word choice, tone of voice, and (sometimes) facial expressions. Releasing the app had made Jarli very unpopular among dishonest people, which had turned out to be just about everyone.

Doug had been especially angry. And now Jarli realized why—Doug Hennessey wasn't even his real name.

If Doug wasn't Doug, who was he?

"Jarli," Bess was saying. "Are you listening?" She and King, the firefighter with the moustache, were staring at him.

Jarli snapped out of it. There was no time to wonder about Doug. "We have to get out of here," he told them. "There's a gas stove in the house."

Bess's eyes widened. "Like, flammable gas? Kaboom gas?"

King held up his gloved hands. "It's okay," he said. "We turned off the gas connection to the house. There's not—"

BOOM!

Blast Radius

The plane turned into a fireball. The rest of Doug's house disintegrated as a shock wave rippled across the street, cracking windows and knocking the leaves off trees. The air hit Jarli like a fist, and he fell onto his back. If he hadn't already been sitting down, the impact could have killed him.

He found himself staring at the tower of smoke against the blue sky, too dizzy to stand up.

"Bess?" he called. "Bess!"

No reply. He could hardly hear anything over the pounding of his heart.

Jarli rolled onto his side. King was lying facedown on the road nearby, not moving.

He said the gas had been shut off, Jarli thought. His mind was whirling. *An empty plane, a false name, an impossible explosion—none of this is right.*

"Bess?" Jarli shouted again.

Her voice floated from somewhere nearby. "I'm okay. Are you?"

Jarli sat up. Bess was on the ground, not far away. It looked like her backpack had broken her fall.

A flood of relief swept through Jarli. Bess had been his best friend since they were toddlers. Losing her was unthinkable.

"I'm fine." He reached over and grabbed the big firefighter's shoulder. "Hey, Mr. King. Can you hear me?"

The firefighter stirred, hands fumbling around on the asphalt. His helmet must have protected his head.

"What happened?" he groaned.

"The house exploded." *Right after you told us it wouldn't,* Jarli thought.

Burning debris rained down on the other houses in the street. Firefighters blasted them and the surrounding trees with huge hoses. Steam filled the air.

Fiona ran over and knelt next to King. "Wesley," she said. "You all right?"

"Yeah, yeah." King shook his head, clearing it.

An ambulance screeched to a halt up the other end of the street. Two paramedics leaped out and ran toward Bess.

Jarli suddenly realized he couldn't see Doug anymore. He twisted around one way and then the other. Doug was gone.

A woman and a man approached Jarli. The woman had a chipped tooth and dark eyes. The man was tall, with white-blond hair, saggy cheeks, and a scar on the back of his hand. They both wore normal clothes, so it took Jarli a minute to recognize them: Constable Irena Blanco and Constable Daniel Frink.

"Jarli Durras," Blanco said, scratching one eyebrow. "Trouble seems to follow you around, doesn't it?"

Jarli felt his face get hot. "This isn't my fault."

"We know." Frink crouched down next to him. "Are you okay?"

"I think so." Jarli wondered why the officers weren't in uniform. Had they been called in on their day off? The only car nearby was an unmarked sedan farther up the street.

"You saw the plane crash," Blanco said. It wasn't a question. "Then you went into the house. We'd like to ask you some questions."

"Just a minute," called one of the paramedics, who ran over to Jarli while his partner was examining Bess. "I need to get a look at him first."

The two cops stood back while the paramedic shone a flashlight in Jarli's eyes. He didn't wait for permission. "How do you feel, Jarli?"

"Fine."

"Can you turn your head this way for me?"

Jarli did. "How do you know my name?"

"We met last year. You were in a car crash. My name's Tyson. Now, this way, please."

Jarli turned his head the other way. "You have a good memory."

"It was memorable." Tyson turned to the police. "His spine and brain are fine. You can take him now."

"Where are you taking him?" Bess asked.

"Jarli didn't hear the response because he'd just realized something strange. Blanco and Frink had seen him run into the house. They had been here before the plane crashed."

Why?

"What did Doug Hennessey say when he arrived at the crash site?" Frink asked.

Jarli frowned. "Why?"

"Just answer the question," Blanco said.

Jarli shrugged. "I don't remember exactly what he said."

They were in an interview room at Kelton Police Department—a small concrete building opposite the town hall, which Jarli had completely ignored until the first time he got dragged in there. The smells of burned coffee and mold lingered in the air. Jarli's chair was about as comfortable as a milk crate. A camera stood in the corner, red light blinking.

Jarli had called his mum on the way here. She'd told him Dad would be there pronto. Her voice had been calm, but Jarli could sense the anxiety behind her words. He got the feeling she would never let him leave the house again. Mum already didn't trust him to stay out of trouble. Even though it wasn't his fault, the plane crash wouldn't have helped.

"You don't remember what he said," Blanco repeated, staring at her phone. "You know, your trust rating isn't great. Seventy-one percent."

Jarli sighed. The police were using a rip-off of his lie-detector app called *Truth Premium*. It cost $0.99 and had some additional, annoying features. It used a voice-print database to identify the person talking, and then adjusted their "trust rating" as it listened. Jarli knew people who spent hours saying true things to their phones in an effort to pump up their average score.

"Let's say we believe you," Blanco said. "Was there anyone else around who might have talked to Doug?"

Jarli didn't know Blanco well, but he could tell she was rattled. Kelton had been plane-crash-free until today. Her questions so far had been all over the place: *Were the engines still running when the plane crashed? Did it turn while it was falling? Was anyone else hanging around the crash site?*

"You tell me," Jarli said. "You were there."

Blanco lifted her chin. "I wasn't."

"You said I went into the house *after* the crash," Jarli said. "How would you know that, if you weren't watching?"

Blanco and Frink looked at each other. Then Blanco reached over and turned off the recorder.

"My partner and I were parked on top of the hill with binoculars," Blanco said. "We didn't see the plane until it hit the building."

"We saw you run in before we hightailed it down the hill," Frink added. "You have guts, kid."

"Why were you up there?" Jarli asked. "What were you looking at?"

Blanco's eyes narrowed, suspicious, and Jarli started to feel guilty, even though he hadn't done anything wrong.

Frink turned the recorder back on. "Let's talk more about Doug."

The police officers seemed to be on edge, and they weren't the only ones. Jarli had checked his phone on the way to the police station, and social media was going nuts.

DN Dale
#Keltoncrash This for real? Was anyone in the house?

RC Ralph
Plane was hacked! North Korean cyberterrorism.
#keltoncrash

IW Izzy@Ralph
Truth!

FS Fred@Ralph
In Kelton???? No way . . .

KD Kristie
#keltoncrash ALIENS
PO Peta
#keltoncrash Is this what Plowman's making? Some kind of torpedo plane?

TL Tom@Peta

Get the weapons out of our town!

CW Chris

some kind of insurance scam #keltoncrash

Everyone had the same basic facts—plane crashes into house in Kelton—but there were hundreds of different theories.

"Did Doug say where he was going?" Blanco asked.

Jarli remembered the way he had disappeared from the street. "I don't think so. Is he missing?"

Blanco ignored the question. "Who does he hang out with at school?"

"No one, really." Doug was kind of a loner.

"Tell me about the inside of the house. Did you see anything out of the ordinary? Papers, photos?"

"I wasn't looking for papers or photos," Jarli said. "I was looking for people. And there was so much smoke I could hardly see anything."

Blanco's face stayed even, but Jarli had the strange sense she was relieved. "Okay. What about the inside of the plane? Did you see the passenger? Or the pilot?"

The passenger. Jarli had thought the plane was empty. But what if he'd missed someone?

"I didn't see anything," he said, trying to keep his voice even.

Blanco scribbled a note and slid her papers back into a

folder. "Well, I think that's everything we need, Mr. Durras."

"Did you find a body?" Jarli asked nervously.

"We'll let you know the results of our investigation."

"Is Doug missing?"

Frink clenched his jaw but said nothing. Maybe he didn't want the app to catch him out.

Blanco glanced at the clock. "Interview terminated at seventeen hundred hours," she said. She passed Jarli a business card. "Call us if you remember something else. And if I were you, I wouldn't tell anyone about anything you saw. Not your friends, not the press. Definitely no posts on social media. Got that?"

Jarli nodded vigorously. They didn't have to tell him not to trust reporters.

He was escorted out of the interview room, confused and exhausted. Through a barred window he could see the sunset, which he thought at first was the sunrise. It felt like he'd been in there all night.

Dad was in the waiting room, cracking his hairy knuckles while he examined a celebrity gossip magazine. The front-page headline screamed *PRINCE MYRON DISGRACED!* in garish yellow font.

"I thought you hated those magazines," Jarli said. "Busted."

"I do!" Dad said defensively, dropping the tabloid. Jarli waited for his phone to beep and then remembered that the cops had made him turn it off before the interview.

Dad hugged Jarli tightly. He smelled like sweat and laundry powder.

"Good to see you in one piece," Dad said gruffly. Then he smiled. "Now, what have you done this time?"

"I'm just a helpful witness," Jarli said gravely, "assisting the authorities with their inquiries."

"Spoken like a true criminal. Come on."

Mum's new car was in the parking lot. The insurance company had finally gotten around to replacing their old car after the crash. It looked like Dad had washed it today, polishing the metallic blue paint and vacuuming the gray floors inside. He had washed it every week since they'd gotten it. Jarli gave this newfound diligence about a month.

Kirstie was in the back seat, still dressed in her soccer gear. "Hey, bro," she said. "I hear you brought down a plane."

"Not me," Jarli said. "Reliable sources tell me that it was aliens."

Kirstie grinned. "You saw that, huh?"

Dad started the car. "I wish you hadn't made that post, Kirstie. It's offensive."

"To who?" Kirstie asked. "Aliens?"

Kelton Town Hall was right across the road from the police station. As they drove out of the parking lot, Jarli noticed that a crowd had gathered on the front steps. Mayor Shelby was making a speech. The people in the crowd wore suits and had perfect hair. A few carried cameras.

Journalists, Jarli thought with a twinge of panic. After his app had gone viral, he'd been followed by every reporter in Kelton and a few from out of town. They had eventually lost interest, but Jarli still couldn't watch the news without getting uncomfortable. He remembered vividly what it was like to be on the other side of the screen.

They're here for the plane crash, he told himself. *Not me.*

One of the journalists turned to face the car: Dana Reynolds, from *Nationwide*. She was the worst of the bunch—she had somehow managed to get Jarli's phone number and kept calling him until he was forced to change it.

Jarli slunk down in his seat, but it was too late. She had seen him. Reynolds's clear green eyes widened. She grabbed the nearest camera operator with a manicured claw and pointed to the car.

Then Dad turned a corner, and the reporters were out of sight. It looked like he was taking the long way home to avoid the commotion here and near the crash site.

"It's offensive to the families of anyone who might have been on the plane," Dad was saying.

"No one was on the plane," Kirstie protested.

"How do *you* know that?" Jarli asked.

"Finn told me after Bess told him what the firefighters had told her."

Jarli groaned. Finn was Bess's little brother. If he knew, so would everyone else in town—and they would start hassling Jarli for more information.

Thanks to the police, Jarli knew that Kirstie was wrong. There had been one passenger. But if he told anyone that, the police would soon realize Jarli had spilled the beans.

Jarli wondered how Bess was doing. He sent her a text message:

Leaving the police station. The cops are clueless. 😟
How are you?

"Well, what about the people who lost their house?" Dad said. "You think they appreciate being joked about?"

Kirstie waved a hand. "Who cares about them?" she said. "That guy deserves it, after he threatened Jarli."

Dad glanced at Jarli in the rearview mirror. "Wait. It was *that* boy's house?"

Jarli glared at Kirstie.

After Dad found out about the incident with Doug, he had wanted Doug to be expelled. Jarli had begged Dad to leave it alone. If the bullies at school thought Jarli couldn't fight his own battles, he would get picked on even more. Dad eventually relented, but Jarli had known he was still angry. Now Kirstie had brought it up again.

"Well," Dad said darkly, "sounds like karma to me."

It didn't feel like karma. Doug had lost his whole house. That was so much worse than anything that had happened to Jarli. And what about Doug's parents? They hadn't done anything wrong.

There was one thing Jarli hadn't told the police: that Doug had lied about his name. Jarli wasn't quite sure why he'd held back. Maybe because Doug's home had been destroyed, and Jarli didn't want to add to his classmate's troubles. Maybe because he wasn't sure the app was right. It was programmed to see nervousness as a sign of dishonesty, and Doug had been frightened for other reasons.

Or maybe because of the strange feeling that Blanco and Frink already knew the truth. In fact—

Jarli didn't get the chance to finish this train of thought. He saw something out the window as the headlights swept across it. A huge piece of cloth, tangled around a tree.

A parachute.

Emergency Landing

S top the car!" Jarli shouted.

Dad slowed. "What?" he said. "What's going on?"

"Stop! I saw something."

The car halted fifty or sixty meters up the road from the parachute. Jarli scrambled out and ran back along the road toward it.

This looked like a better place for an emergency landing than Mickle Street. No houses, no streetlights. Just paddocks on one side of the road and bush on the other, lit by the red glow of Dad's brake lights. Dry grass and weeds threatened to take over the asphalt. Jarli wondered why the pilot hadn't tried to land the plane here.

In the moonlight, the parachute looked like a beached jellyfish. The thick silk canopy was thoroughly tangled in the branches of the tree. Nylon ropes swayed underneath in the breeze.

Jarli had been afraid that he would see a dead body hanging from the chute. But no. The harness was there, empty. Someone had escaped.

Jarli whipped out his phone and refreshed his feed, trying to find a mention of survivors. There was nothing.

Maybe the police didn't know yet. Blanco hadn't mentioned anyone. But the crash was hours ago. Why hadn't the survivor contacted anyone? And where were they?

Jarli had the sudden feeling that he was being watched. He turned around, unnerved.

The forest stared back at him, dark and restless. Gum trees swayed like zombies, leaves muttering.

Maybe the survivor had amnesia. They could have bumped their head and wandered off. That might explain why they hadn't gone to the police. Or maybe the survivor was a criminal. Maybe they had even caused the crash—

A hand fell on Jarli's shoulder.

Jarli yelped. But it was just Dad.

"Jarli," he said. "What's going on?"

"Don't sneak up on me like that," Jarli said, his heart still racing.

"I called your name several times," Dad said. This was probably true. When Jarli was coding or wrapped up in his own thoughts, he often didn't hear people talking to him.

Jarli pointed at the parachute. "Look."

Dad stared at the chute for a moment. The wind billowed under the canvas.

"Well," he said uneasily, "at least we know someone survived."

"But why haven't they called the police?" Jarli asked. "Or walked back to Kelton?"

"Maybe they're hurt." Dad cupped his hands around his mouth. "Hello?"

His voice echoed through the dark bush. There was no reply.

Kirstie was standing behind Dad. "Maybe aliens took them," she whispered.

"Kirstie," Jarli sighed. But the idea seemed less silly now than it had in the daylight.

"Call the police," Dad told Jarli finally. "I'm going to have a look around."

"Don't leave us," Jarli said, hating how anxious he sounded.

"It's okay," Dad said. "I'm not going far."

He walked into the trees, scanning the ground for the injured survivor. Jarli dialed Constable Blanco. He had her number saved into his phone.

She picked up quickly. "Blanco speaking."

"It's Jarli Durras."

"Jarli. What can I do for you?"

"Dad was driving me home, and I saw a parachute in a tree," Jarli said. "We're on the highway."

Dad had disappeared into the trees. Jarli hoped he was still within earshot.

"I know," Blanco said. "We've traced the call. I can see your location on my screen. No sign of the pilot?"

"No."

"Okay. I'm coming now. But I think you and your dad should get back in the car and keep driving, okay?"

"Why?" The hairs on the back of Jarli's neck were standing up.

"It's not safe. Head home, and send me a text when you get there."

"What's going on?"

"Just trust me."

The line went dead.

Dad still hadn't returned.

"Dad?" Jarli called.

No answer. The trees seemed somehow taller, and the shadows deeper. An owl hooted in the distance.

"Dad!" Jarli squeaked.

Then Dad emerged from the trees.

"No sign of anyone," he said.

The bush whispered secrets, too soft to make out.

Wall of Fame

When they got home, Dad opened the triple-locked front door and then immediately disappeared into his study to make a call. A former data network engineer, Dad now freelanced for companies all over the world. He was often up at odd hours, talking to one person on the phone while he typed instant messages to several others. Jarli had no idea how he kept track of so many conversations at once.

But it was better than Dad's last job, which had made him a target of Viper.

Viper was a crime boss, real name unknown. The police didn't even know what he or she looked like. But they knew Viper was ruthless, and skilled at making people disappear—allies and enemies alike. Viper had used an assassin with the code-name "Cobra" to try to kill Dad. Jarli helped the police catch him, but Cobra had vanished from his prison cell. A note had been left behind: a message for Jarli, warning him not to interfere with Viper's business.

After that, Mum and Dad installed a back-to-base alarm and security mesh over all the windows. But Jarli still found it hard to sleep. Every time the house creaked or the fence rattled in the middle of the night, Jarli would lurch upright, heart pounding—terrified that the next morning his parents would open the door to find his bed empty.

"We're back," Jarli called.

Hooper ran up and sniffed his shoes. She hadn't been walked much lately. Everyone in the family was anxious about leaving the house alone.

Mum emerged from the kitchen and hugged him. "I hear you ran into a burning building." She looked Jarli over, checking him for any injuries.

"It was more like a *missing* building," Jarli told her. "There was only one wall left."

"That was very brave, and your father and I are proud of you," Mum said. "But do me a favor, mate. Next time, leave it to the authorities."

"But what if someone had been trapped?"

"They weren't."

"Yeah, but they could have been," Jarli said. "You think I should have done nothing?"

"You should have called the fire department."

"I did. Well, Bess did."

"I get what you're saying," Mum said, hugging him again. "But I don't want you to put yourself in danger. Even if you're doing it to help someone else. Wait for the police or the fire brigade, okay?"

"I understand," Jarli said, and he did. But he was glad Mum didn't make him promise, because he wasn't sure it was a promise he could keep. When the plane hit the house, he hadn't actually decided to run over—he had just done it. Helping wasn't just what he did, it was who he was. He couldn't turn that off.

"I'm gonna work on the Wall," he said.

"Dinner's in ten minutes," Mum warned.

Jarli nodded and escaped into his bedroom.

When *Truth* went viral, Jarli became a target for journalists and trolls. So he'd frantically started researching cybersecurity, trying to improve his online privacy and keep his personal devices safe.

He soon became fascinated. There was a secret world beneath the Internet—an army of criminals constantly attacking electronic devices, and an equally determined army of security personnel protecting those devices. Both sides were so good at their jobs that more than 99 percent of those attacks went unnoticed.

Jarli had started developing his own firewall, designed to keep hackers and viruses out of his network. Maybe someday it would work well enough that he could share it. Then he wouldn't just be known as the *Truth*-app guy anymore.

But to test it, he needed some viruses. Really nasty ones.

Jarli booted up his laptop. It was a cheap, slow contraption he had found in a secondhand store. Viper and Cobra had stolen his old computer, along with the TV, Kirstie's diary, and plenty of other stuff. That meant they probably knew everything about Jarli and his family now.

The bright side was that the new laptop had none of Jarli's data on it. It was expendable. He used it like a crash-test dummy, downloading things that would have been too dangerous to put on his old PC.

Booting up the laptop took forever. A real computer whiz might have been able to crack open the casing and upgrade the RAM or processor to make the computer run faster. But Jarli was just a programmer. He understood lines of code, but the actual wires and circuits were a mystery.

Jarli made sure WallOfFame was running, then he opened a browser and visited a hacker forum where he'd seen a promising virus.

There it was: OUROBOROS.

The virus was disguised as a free photo editor with cool filters. Once it was downloaded and installed, it would scan the computer's hard drive and silently, invisibly upload a copy of almost every file to a server in India. Then it would erase all traces of itself. The hacker who had written it bragged that it couldn't be detected or stopped by four of the top five antivirus programs.

Jarli clicked download.

WallOfFame objected immediately.

File name: picsaver.exe

WARNING: This file may be unsafe. The code requests permissions not normally granted to this sort of program. It is not recommended that you continue.

Jarli rubbed his hands together. His firewall was working, at least on incoming traffic. But what if the virus arrived via a USB port rather than an Internet connection? Would the firewall notice?

Jarli turned off WallOfFame, plugged in a flash drive that he kept on his key ring, and downloaded OUROBOROS onto it. Then he turned the firewall back on and tried to install OUROBOROS.

Success—which meant failure. WallOfFame hadn't noticed the danger. The virus was uploading his whole hard drive, and Jarli's firewall thought everything was fine.

Jarli sighed, unplugged the flash drive, and disconnected his computer from the Wi-Fi. WallOfFame still needed a lot of work.

His phone chimed. Finally, a message from Bess:

I'm fine. The police interrogation took FOREVER. Frink seemed nice, but Blanco looked like she was itching to arrest me for something.

Another message came through.

> But I'm missing a bolt from one of my crutches. I just leaned on it and it collapsed.

Jarli wrote back:

> Jeez, you OK?

> I'm fine, but I need to fix it. It takes me forever to walk anywhere. I'm going crazy. 😠 I think it must have come out when I fell over after the explosion. You didn't pick it up, did you?

> I didn't see it. But Mum has spare bolts. What size do you need?

> No, it's a special one. It has a funny shape, and it'll be expensive to replace. Maybe tomorrow you could help me look for it?

She sent a GIF of a cat with its front paws together, pleading.

Jarli hesitated. Then he wrote:

> Tomorrow might be too late. The police cleanup crew are probably there right now. They might chuck it away.

> 🙁

> We could go there tonight.

> In the dark? 😮

> We should at least try. Hang on.

Jarli walked back into the kitchen. He could see through to the lounge room, where the news was on the TV. Firefighters were hosing down the crashed plane in the destroyed house. A photo of a dark-eyed woman in a pilot's uniform flashed up on the screen.

"The search for the pilot, Priya Lekis, is ongoing," the journalist said gravely. "I'm Dana Reynolds, and you're watching *Nationwide*."

As the camera cut to Reynolds sitting at the news desk, a graphic of the *Truth Premium* logo appeared with some text at the bottom of the screen.

Check out our 100% trust rating!

Even journalists were using the rip-off of Jarli's app now.

Jarli tore his eyes away from the screen. "Mum, can I take my dinner to Bess's place?"

"Why?" Mum asked. "You know I don't like you going out alone at night." She sounded annoyed, but she was already getting two Tupperware containers from the cupboard.

Jarli doubted that Mum would respond well if he said he was going to the crash site. But he couldn't lie with all these phones in the room. Everyone had his app installed.

"It's not even six o'clock yet," he said. True. "And we never got to watch *Snake Man 3*." Also true. "I'm hoping I won't be out too late if I go now." True.

He waited to see if the app would beep. It would have detected from the pitch of his voice that he was nervous, even though he was telling the truth. But the phone camera couldn't see his face, so it couldn't measure his pupil dilation and detect that he was concentrating on hiding some of the facts. And he didn't think his choice of words was evasive enough to set off the alarms he'd programmed.

All the phones in the room remained silent. But Hooper tilted her head, confused. She could tell something was up. No app was as good as Jarli's dog when it came to spotting deception.

Mum started scooping vegetarian lasagna into the containers. "Okay. Take some for Bess, too," she said. "And call if you need a lift home. I don't want you walking the streets in the dark."

"All right," Jarli said. He told himself not to feel guilty. He'd be back in no time, safe and sound.

Crash Site

A smoky haze still lingered in the air, smudging the glow from the streetlights and stinging Jarli's nose. The plane's belly had left a scar at least forty meters long down the middle of the road.

The shell of the wrecked aircraft lay in the ruins of Doug Hennessey's house like the skeleton of a whale. The fire had hollowed out the cabin, burning away the seats and turning the compact kitchen to ash.

The reporters were gone—it was too dark to film anything now. There were no police cars either, just a brown four-wheel drive and a black van parked nearby. Yellow crime-scene tape stretched from what was left of a power pole to a letterbox on the other side of the street. The tape fluttered in the breeze, but Jarli could still read the message: POLICE LINE. DO NOT CROSS.

Jarli pedaled toward the crime-scene tape. Bess was behind him, her arms around his waist. Jarli and his sister rode like this all the time, but it was harder with Bess, because she had to carry her crutches. They had only tried it once before, when their friend Anya had been held hostage by Cobra. Now Jarli was struggling to balance. He hoped the jolting of the road hadn't shaken out any more bolts or screws from her crutches.

The brakes squeaked as Jarli's bicycle rattled to a stop. "Well," he said, "that's that." He had lied to Mum for nothing.

"What do you mean?" Bess carefully maneuvered herself off his bicycle and leaned her broken crutch against it.

Jarli gestured to the police tape. "We can't go in."

"No, it's easy," Bess said. "You just lift it up. See?"

She held up the police tape.

"You know what I mean," Jarli said. "What if they blocked it off because of toxic fumes or something?"

"Then they would have evacuated the neighbors." Bess pointed at the second-story window of the nearest house, which had lights on.

"Oh, great. So people will *see* us sneaking into a crime scene. You've got a screw loose."

"Ha, ha." Bess dug out her phone and brought up a flashlight app. "We're witnesses. We're allowed to be here."

"I'm ninety percent sure that's not how it works," Jarli said. But he followed her under the tape anyway and switched on his own flashlight app. The sooner they found the bolt, the sooner they could get out of here.

They both swept their lights across the road. Broken glass sparkled like stars.

"What does it look like?" Jarli asked.

"It's about five centimeters long, maybe? Gray. One end is sharp, the other is hexagonal."

"So, like a bolt, in other words."

"Yup. But with a sharp end."

Jarli peered at the road. Even in daylight, this would be an impossible task. The road was strewn with shrapnel after the crash. It was like looking for a needle in a haystack. A haystack made of needles.

"Maybe we should ask those guys for help," Bess said.

"Which guys?" Then Jarli saw movement inside the gutted airplane. A flashlight beam flitting through the smashed windows. As his eyes adjusted, he saw what Bess had seen—two men dressed head-to-toe in airtight plastic, gas masks covering their faces. Jarli wondered again if it was dangerous to be here, breathing the air.

One of the men was picking things out of the ashes and putting them into a big garbage bag. The other was sweeping a device across the floor, scanning. It looked like a walking stick, but with a ring as large as a dinner plate on the bottom end. They hadn't seen the two teenagers yet.

"Is that a metal detector?" Jarli asked. Dad had rented one when he lost his wedding ring in the backyard. It hadn't worked for Dad, but maybe it would work for Bess.

"Looks like one. I'll go ask if we can borrow it." Bess limped slowly toward the plane. Walking with only one crutch looked painful, but Bess had told Jarli many times that her legs didn't actually hurt. They just never did quite what her brain told them to.

"Wait," Jarli said. "Remember, we're not supposed to be here."

Bess waved a hand. "Relax. It'll be fine."

She was used to people doing what she wanted. Too used to it, Jarli sometimes thought.

The two men seemed to have found what they were looking for. The one scanning pointed to something that looked like a data projector, and the one bagging picked it up. It was the same mysterious object Jarli had seen when he searched Doug's house. The firefighters must have moved it.

Maybe it was the black box—the indestructible device that recorded flight data in case of a crash. It was weird that it had taken the police so long to find it. Maybe the gas explosion had buried it under some more rubble.

Or maybe "Scanner" and "Bagger" weren't with the police.

Dread grew in Jarli's belly. There were no police cars on the street. The hazmat suits were dark gray, not designed to stand out. The two men didn't want to be seen.

"Wait," Jarli hissed again. But Bess was already shuffling through the gap where the plane's emergency exit had once been.

Then it was too late.

The two men spotted Bess at the same moment. They

froze as they saw her standing in the doorway.

"Excuse me," Bess said, oblivious to the danger. "Can I borrow—"

"Grab her, grab her!" Scanner shouted, his voice muffled by the gas mask.

Bagger lunged toward Bess. She stumbled backward, shocked. Bagger was weighed down by his suit, but with only one working crutch, Bess had no hope of outrunning him. She screamed as Bagger reached out to grab her.

But as Scanner tried to move the metal detector out of the way, he accidentally tripped Bagger.

"Idiot!" Bagger yelled in midair. His head thumped against one of the charred seats, and he hit the floor like a bag of potatoes. It would have been funny if Jarli hadn't been so scared.

Jarli ran into the airplane and grabbed Bess. The floor was shredded. The ashes of the furniture felt like slush under his feet. Bess's legs were twitching. The spasms got worse when she was stressed.

Jarli was about to drag her to her feet when Scanner swung the metal detector at Jarli's head.

If the strike connected, it would crack his skull. But Scanner swung it slowly, like it was heavy. Jarli ducked, and the metal detector swooshed through the air centimeters above his head.

Jarli didn't give him time for another try. He stayed low

and charged forward, crashing into Scanner's chest. They both went down, kicking up a cloud of ash as they hit the floor next to Bess.

Heart pounding, Jarli tried to wrestle the metal detector out of Scanner's hands, but his grip was too strong. He could see Scanner's eyes, narrowed with anger behind the transparent plastic of his mask.

Bess grabbed the garbage bag and pulled it over Scanner's head, blinding him. The bag was so big that it covered most of his torso as well.

Scanner struggled frantically, but the bag was made of tough polyvinyl, and his arms were all tangled up inside. It would take him a few seconds to fight his way out. Bagger still hadn't gotten up.

"Come on!" Jarli hissed. He pulled Bess up. She wrapped her arm around his shoulders and they hobbled out of the airplane together, three-legged-race style. They had to move slowly to avoid stumbling on the broken bricks that had once been Doug's home.

It was about fifteen meters to the crime-scene tape, and maybe another five to Jarli's bike. Not far, but even with his clumsy hazmat suit, Scanner would be faster than them.

"Hurry," Bess hissed.

"I *am* hurrying!" Jarli snapped back. They were almost at the crime-scene tape now.

Jarli could hear movement from inside the plane. As they

ducked under the tape, he risked a glance back.

Scanner was still struggling with the garbage bag on his head. Something Mum often said flashed through Jarli's head: *He couldn't find his way out of a wet paper bag.*

But Bagger—the man who had tripped and hit his head— had gotten up. He turned around, looking for them.

"On the bike!" Jarli whispered. "Quick!"

Bagger spotted them as they limped toward the bicycle. He ran through the emergency exit, out of the ruins of Doug's house, and sprinted toward them.

Jarli jumped onto the bike. Bess clambered on behind him, jammed both crutches between them, and held on tight.

"Go, go!" she said.

Bagger was getting closer. His hazmat suit hissed like a wave approaching the shore. Jarli started pedaling, Bess clinging to his waist. First gear, second gear. The bike gained speed. Third gear.

Then it stopped suddenly. Jarli felt himself wrenched backward as Bess screamed. Bagger had grabbed her hair.

"Got you," he snarled.

Reluctant Allies

Bess and Jarli toppled off the bike. The asphalt bit Jarli's elbow and knee as he rolled sideways. By the time he scrambled to his feet, Bagger had Bess's wrist clenched in one hand and her hair in the other. He was holding her at arm's length so she couldn't hit him with her free hand.

"Get off me!" she shrieked. She tried to kick him, but Bagger dodged easily. He wasn't as clumsy as Scanner.

"Stay back," Bagger told Jarli. The gas mask turned his voice into an alien growl.

Jarli's body was a coiled spring. Maybe he and Bess could overpower the man together.

Bagger released Bess's hair and grabbed her throat instead. "Back," he warned. "Or I'll crush her windpipe."

Bess's eyes were huge with fear.

Jarli took a slow step backward.

"Who do you work for?" Bagger asked.

"No one," Jarli said. "We're just kids."

"Did Fussell send you?"

"I don't know what you're talking about."

"Tell me—*hurgh!*"

Bagger went rigid. He trembled, almost vibrating. Then he tipped sideways, as stiff as a broom. Bess wriggled out of his grip just in time to avoid being dragged down with him.

Bagger hit the road and lay still. Jarli couldn't work out what had happened—until he saw Doug Hennessey.

Doug was standing right behind Bagger, holding something that looked like a phone. Then Jarli noticed two prongs protruding from one end. It was a stun gun. Doug had given Bagger an electric shock.

A bunch of questions tried to come out of Jarli's mouth at once. Why was Doug here? Was that even his real name? Where had he been? Why did he have a stun gun? Who were the men in hazmat suits?

"What?" Jarli heard himself say.

"This thing has a high voltage, but not much current," Doug said, holding up the stun gun. "He'll be up in a minute. Come on, we have to hide!"

Dazed, Jarli put his arm around Bess's shoulders, helping her limp after Doug. Doug grabbed the crutches and wheeled the bike behind the old brown four-wheel drive in the neighbor's driveway. The three of them crouched down.

"We can't stay here," Bess whispered. "They'll find us."

"They're not going to hang around," Doug said. "Mr. Lewis saw the whole thing. He called the cops."

He pointed at the house with the lit window. Jarli could hear sirens on the breeze.

He hoped Doug was right, because it was too late to flee. Heavy footsteps were approaching.

Jarli lay on the concrete driveway, peering under the four-wheel drive. He saw Scanner—the guy Bess had trapped in the bag—emerge from the crashed plane and run over to his stunned colleague. He was carrying the blackened box and a small flashlight.

Scanner crouched down and leaned in, checking that Bagger was still breathing. Apparently, the hazmat suits made it too hard to tell. He pulled off his hood and Bagger's, too.

This gave Jarli a good look at Scanner—he had a square nose, curly brown hair, and dark circles around his eyes. From this angle, Jarli couldn't see Bagger's face, just a mess of blond hair.

Scanner peeled off a glove and checked Bagger's pulse. Then he looked around at the quiet street. Jarli kept perfectly still against the concrete, not even daring to breathe.

Apparently satisfied, Scanner picked Bagger up, and carried him over to the black van parked nearby. Jarli watched as he lifted Bagger into the passenger seat and buckled him in. Then he climbed into the driver's side and drove away.

Doug exhaled. "We have to get out of here before the cops show up," he whispered.

"*What?*" Bess demanded. "Why?"

"The bad guys are tracking police communications somehow. If the police find out who we are, those two will hear about it. They'll find us and kill us. We know too much."

"We don't know anything," Jarli said.

"We know enough." Doug stood up. "Come on."

"You're full of it," Bess said. "The police can protect us. I'm not running away."

"The police were supposed to be protecting me," Doug said. "Then a plane crashed into my house."

"We're not going anywhere with you."

"Fine. Stay. But I won't save you a second time. Nice knowing you." Doug started walking away.

"You threatened Jarli," Bess snarled. "Why would we trust you?"

"You don't need to trust me," Doug said. "What does your app say, Jarli?"

Jarli realized that his phone hadn't beeped once during this conversation. He unlocked it and checked that *Truth* was running. It was.

Jarli felt off balance, as though the rotation of the Earth had changed direction under his feet. Doug believed everything that he was saying. Either he was crazy, or they were in terrible danger.

The sirens were getting louder. "Are you coming, or what?" Doug asked.

Jarli hesitated. "Who were those men?"

"They work for a seriously bad guy."

"Who?"

"I don't know his real name," Doug said. "But people call him Viper."

Call Me Mr. Smith

Terence was building a robot when his world ended.

It wasn't a complicated machine. Basically just a battering ram with two wheels and a radio antenna. Despite this, Terence was struggling to get it working. The battery wasn't providing enough charge, so he'd tried plugging it into a wall socket. But then the robot kept getting tangled up in its own power cable. He couldn't even drive it from one side of his bedroom to the other.

"You're *so* dead," said Rebecca in his earpiece.

"Like you're doing any better," Terence grumbled. Rebecca was bugging him, but later he would remember this as the last time he had been happy.

"*My* robot is working fine," Rebecca continued. "She's gonna smash yours. You'll have to take a garbage bag to the championship to collect all the pieces."

"If you're trying to psych me out, it's not working."

"Just stating the facts." Terence could hear Rebecca drilling something in the background. "Chloe's a guaranteed winner. Iris and I painted her pink—the color of *victory*.

You may as well quit now and save yourself the entry fee."

Terence frowned. "Who's Iris?"

"Just a friend of mine."

Yet another friend. Back when they were little kids, it had been just the two of them. Now they were teenagers, and Terence had to share Rebecca with a seemingly endless bunch of people. Which wouldn't be so bad, except that Terence somehow hadn't made any new friends of his own.

"You called your robot Chloe?" he said. "That's dumb."

"Oh, is it? What's yours called again?"

Terence had named his robot Sir Ramington the Third—there had been two previous versions. He'd been working on it nonstop all weekend. His dad was traveling, and his mum seemed more and more preoccupied lately. She had taken to spreading files across the dinner table and shooing Terence away when he came into the room. She would leave the house unexpectedly and not come back until late at night. She had forbidden Terence from answering the house phone.

With both his parents distracted, Terence wondered if he could get away with skipping school. The Robattle championship was in two weeks—hundreds of robots from all over the country would come to compete. Sir Ramington still wasn't working, so the extra time would be handy.

And school was the worst. The teachers never taught him anything useful. The other kids were mean. And Rebecca, who used to live next door to him, now went to a posh school for girls on the other side of the city, so she wasn't there to make it fun. Maybe she would be willing to skip too.

Terence was trying to think of something clever to say to Rebecca when his mother knocked and walked in without waiting for an answer.

"Turn that thing off," she said, gesturing to the robot. "We need to talk."

Terence fiddled with the controller, trying to reverse Sir Ramington out of the tangled power cord. "Just a second," he said.

"No. Right now." Mum pulled the plug out of the wall. The power light on Sir Ramington went dark.

Terence dropped the controller. "Mum!" This was just like her. Ignoring him for weeks, and then demanding his attention just when he was in the middle of something.

"Come with me," Mum said.

"You can't just . . ." Terence's voice died when he saw the look on his mum's face. It was like the time she got food poisoning— her freckles had gone pale, and her green eyes were bloodshot.

"What's going on?" he asked.

"Come on." Mum walked out of the room without checking that he was following.

"Everything okay?" Rebecca was still on the line.

"Uh, I'll call you back," Terence told her, and hung up.

He never called her back.

• • •

When Terence entered the lounge room, a strange man in a suit and tie was sitting at the dining table. Three manila folders were stacked in front of him, and he was scratching a scar on his hand. The man smiled at Terence, but the smile didn't reach his eyes.

"How much have you told him?" the man asked Mum.

Mum just shook her head, her fist pressed against her mouth.

A chill ran down Terence's spine. "Who are you?"

"You can call me Mr. Smith," the man said. "I'm here to take you somewhere safe."

"What do you mean? What's not safe about here?"

"Someone has threatened your mother."

"Who?" Terence asked.

"Someone dangerous. We have to get both of you out of harm's way, immediately."

Terence looked from Mum to Smith and back again. Maybe this was a prank. Maybe Smith was an old friend of Mum's who liked practical jokes.

"You'll need to pack a bag," Smith said. "It's a long drive. One change of clothes will do, but make sure it's warm. We leave in ten minutes."

"Ten minutes? But—"

"Just clothes. Leave everything else behind."

Terence's phone buzzed. He checked the screen—it was a text from Rebecca.

What's going on? Did I hurt your feelings? 😊

"Don't respond to that, whatever it is," Smith said. "You'll have to leave your phone with me. Viper could be tracking it."

"What's Viper?"

"Just do as he says," Mum told Terence, her voice wobbling. "I'll explain on the way. But everything will be okay, I promise."

Smith held out his hand for the phone.

Terence reluctantly gave it to him. "When are we coming back?" he asked.

No one answered his question, and that gave him a very bad feeling.

"Will we be here when Dad comes back?" Dad wasn't supposed to be flying home until Friday night.

"Your father is going to meet us there." Mum glanced at Smith, who nodded.

"Meet us where?"

"Somewhere safe."

"But when are we coming back?" Terence asked again.

"When it's safe," Smith said. "One more thing." He slid one of the manila folders across the table. "Pack this into your bag. There's no time to go through it now. You'll need to memorize the contents while we're on the road."

Terence took the folder, feeling sick. *Memorize?* This was

like a mash-up of an exam, a TV show, and a bad dream.

"Go," Mum said. "Pack your bag. Quick."

Terence went back to his bedroom, more confused than ever. He emptied out his schoolbag and opened the closet. He grabbed some comfortable pants, a hoodie, and his favorite T-shirt from the pile. He was leaving several other favorite T-shirts on the pile, and he had the sudden terrible feeling that he would never see them again.

And what about Sir Ramington? Could he take the robot with him?

Terence stuffed the clothes into the bag. He was about to put the manila folder in too, when he hesitated. They were in a hurry. But he was scared. He needed to know what was going on.

He opened the folder.

Inside he found a few pictures of himself. School photos, a mug shot from his student ID card, and some pictures from last Christmas. But the mug shot had a different boy's details underneath. A different mobile number. A different e-mail. An address in a town he'd never heard of: Kelton.

And a different name: Douglas Hennessey.

Exposure

Doug took Jarli and Bess to a bridge that crossed Kelton Creek, and then led them down a bumpy grass slope to the darkness beneath the underpass. Bess rode the bike with him. Jarli was on foot, struggling for breath.

The space under the bridge smelled like earth and damp concrete. It was low enough that Jarli had to stoop. Rather than providing shelter from the wind, the bridge seemed to focus it, blasting Jarli with a nonstop wall of cold. The trickling of the creek echoed off concrete walls stained with unreadable graffiti. A pile of broken pallets and flattened cardboard stood nearby.

"Okay," Doug said, climbing off the bike. "Viper has no reason to look for us here. The bridge will hide us from drones and satellites. We'll be safe, for a while."

"From Viper, maybe." Bess hugged herself, teeth chattering. "I give it about two hours before we freeze to death."

Doug lifted one of the broken pallets, revealing a round hole in the wall of the underpass. It was just wide enough for a person to crawl into.

Jarli stared. He and his family had lived here forever. He could draw a detailed map of Kelton, even blindfolded. It was surreal to find a place he'd never noticed before.

"Bilbo Baggins!" Doug called.

His voice bounced away through the tunnel. There was no response.

Jarli and Bess looked at each other.

"That was a password," Doug said gloomily. "When I first moved to Kelton with Mum and Dad, we didn't entirely trust the police. Viper can get to anyone. So we secretly rented a storage unit and filled it with supplies in case something happened and we needed to move again."

"Something like a plane crash?" Jarli asked.

"Not what we expected, but yeah," Doug said. "Unfortunately, the only storage facility in Kelton was too far from the house the Feds gave us. We needed a meeting place. Somewhere we could hide until nightfall without anyone finding us." He gestured at the hole in the wall. "This old mining tunnel was the best we could find. Come on."

He crawled into the hole. After a moment's hesitation, Jarli followed.

The hole opened out to a long chamber with a lumpy stone floor and a low ceiling. It wasn't really a tunnel anymore—the far end had collapsed. Boulders and dirt blocked it off from the other mining tunnels under Kelton. Moss grew in the cracks.

Doug looked around hopefully. But other than a couple of cardboard boxes in the corner, Jarli couldn't see any sign that anyone had been hiding out here.

Bess tossed her crutches through the hole and crawled into the chamber after them. "Wow, nice place you have here," she said.

Doug ignored this. "What were you guys doing at the crash site?"

"Looking for part of Bess's crutches," Jarli said, before Bess could shush him.

"Oh." Doug's gaze settled on the slot where the missing bolt was supposed to be. "Can I see that?"

"Why?" Bess asked suspiciously.

"Maybe I can fix it."

"I doubt it." But she handed the crutch over.

Doug squinted at the hole in the side. Then he tore a damp strip of cardboard off the nearest box, rolled it into a tube, and packed it in.

"If it could be fixed that way, I would have done it myself," Bess said. "Cardboard won't be strong enough."

"I know. I'm just trying to work out the shape." Doug pulled the cardboard back out and examined it carefully.

"Are you going to tell us what's going on?" Jarli asked.

Doug opened his mouth and then hesitated. "Turn your phone off first," he said.

Bess raised an eyebrow. "So you can lie?"

"So no one else can listen in. For all I know, your phones have been hacked."

Jarli's phone didn't beep. Doug was right—any phone with an Internet connection could be used as a recording or listening device.

"I promise I will tell you the truth," Doug added.

Jarli's phone didn't beep, so he turned it off. So did Bess.

"Okay," Doug said. "So, you already know that Doug Hennessey isn't my real name."

"We do?" Bess said.

Jarli nodded. "When he told the firefighter his name, my app said he was lying."

"I knew it," Doug said bitterly. "Your app put my whole family in danger. It was only a matter of time before someone found out."

"Found what out?" Bess said. "What's going on?"

Jarli had already figured it out. "He's in witness protection," he said. "Aren't you?"

Doug nodded. He broke a piece of wood off one of the pallets. "I won't tell you my real name, or where I really come from. If you don't know, then you don't have to keep it a secret. No one can keep a secret anymore, thanks to you."

"Yeah, yeah," Bess said. "We get it: You're mad at Jarli. Get to the point. Why are you in witness protection? What did you do?"

"I didn't do anything. The cops sent me here because of my mum. She used to work for Magnotech."

"The magnet company?" Jarli asked. He knew about Magnotech because they had a factory just north of town, and they had released an unintentionally funny television ad. Jarli and his friends had spent days laughing at it.

Bess did an impression of the guy from the ad: "We're *magnanimous!*"

"That's them," Doug said. "But they don't just sell fridge magnets and door latches. They also make high-end, experimental magnets. The kind they use in bullet trains and MRI scanners. Anyway, Mum worked in one of their offices. It was her job to schedule meetings between buyers, sales reps, and engineers in various countries." As Doug talked, he pulled a pocketknife out of the cardboard box and started hacking at the broken piece of wood. A pile of splinters formed at his feet.

"Viper contacted Magnotech via e-mail," Doug continued, "with a false name. He wanted them to design some kind of magnetic laser device. He requested a particular engineer, who built a prototype. Viper picked it up from one of the factories. A few days after the job was finished, the engineer turned up dead."

The wind howled like ghosts outside.

"How?" Bess asked.

"Officially it was a heart attack."

"And unofficially?"

"The police found an RFID chip embedded in his hand.

It's the same kind of chip they put in credit cards, phones, whatever. Most engineers at Magnotech get one implanted so they can prove their identity when working on secret projects. It's a kind of ID that no one can steal."

Jarli winced. He wanted to work in the tech industry someday, but he didn't like the idea of his boss implanting something under his skin.

"This particular chip," Doug continued, "wasn't the same as the ones the other employees had. There was a fluid capsule built in. The police thought it might have been used to poison him."

The hairs stood up on the back of Jarli's neck. "You think Viper implanted a poison capsule in the engineer's hand? And then triggered it once the prototype of the device was finished?"

Doug nodded. "Covering his tracks. He must have someone else working at the company who swapped the chips the last time the engineer got his implant replaced. The police said that another one of Viper's enemies died the same way soon after. That was how they guessed it was him."

"What does this have to do with your mum?" Bess asked.

"She set up the meetings between Viper and the engineer. So she was the only person left alive who knew for sure where Viper had been, and when. The police thought that was enough to make her a target."

Bess wrapped the coat more tightly around herself. "So what did the police do?"

Doug kept his eyes on the knife in his hands. "They took away our names and gave us new ones. My dad had to quit his job. He was mad about that, I think. I never got the chance to say good-bye to any of my friends. It's been a year since then. I don't know what they think happened to me."

Doug looked away. Jarli thought he might have been trying not to cry.

"The cops sent us to the middle of nowhere so we'd be safe while they investigated," Doug continued. "And then we heard nothing. For a year. I was starting to think I'd never get to go back."

Jarli didn't like hearing his hometown referred to as "nowhere." "Does your mum still work for Magnotech?" he asked. "At the factory in Kelton?"

"No, she works in the mayor's office. Why?"

"Just wondering." It seemed like a weird coincidence that the police had moved Doug's family to a town that had a Magnotech factory. But it was a big company. Jarli supposed they had buildings in a lot of places.

"And then a plane crashed into your new house?" he asked.

"Right. We would all be dead right now if Mum hadn't been asked to stay back late at her new job. That meant Dad had to catch the bus home from work, and I had to walk home from school. When I got back, my whole house was gone. All my books, my game console, my robots . . ." His voice was flat. "For the second time in a year, I lost everything."

"You don't think it's just a coincidence?" Jarli asked hopefully. He didn't want to believe that Viper was still active.

Doug glared at him. "Are you a moron? The plane was empty. The pilot set a course for my house and then bailed out. This was a deliberate attack."

"There must be a less obvious way of killing someone," Bess said.

"I think Viper wanted it to be obvious. He wanted news coverage. He was showing off. Saying, 'This is how easily I can find the people who cross me.'"

"How do you know Viper is tracking police communications?" Jarli asked.

"No one else knew who we were. Our new address was top secret."

"Better stop blaming Jarli, then," Bess said. "If the police leaked your location, then it's nothing to do with the app."

Doug opened his mouth, then closed it again.

"If you can't go to the police," Jarli asked finally, "what are you going to do?"

Doug wiped his nose on his sleeve. "I came straight here after the crash. A few hours later, Mum and Dad still hadn't shown up, so I went back to the house to look for them. They weren't there, so they must still be on their way here. I just have to wait."

Jarli and Bess looked at each other. That sounded like wishful thinking. If Doug's parents were coming, they would have been here by now.

"You mentioned a storage locker," Bess said. "Maybe they went straight there."

"No. That wasn't the plan. We're supposed to meet here."

"You can't just stay here, though. What will you eat?"

Doug opened the cardboard box and started rummaging through it. "There's some granola bars somewhere in here."

"You can't live off those," Bess said. "You'll get scurvy."

"That's weird." Doug stopped rummaging. "I can't find them."

"Have some of this." Jarli dug the lasagna containers out of his bag and passed them to Doug. "Still warm."

"Thanks." Before Doug opened a container, he held out the piece of wood he had been carving. Jarli realized it was the same shape as the missing bolt from the crutch.

Bess took it, frowning. "That's . . . amazing," she said finally.

"Don't thank me yet. It might not work."

Bess pushed the bolt into the hole. It looked a bit stiff, but it fit. She leaned on her crutch, and it held.

"Wow," she said. "Thank you."

Doug shrugged and started eating the lasagna. He didn't have any plates or cutlery, so he ate directly out of the container with his dirty hands. He looked like a stray animal.

"Excuse us," Bess said, and dragged Jarli back over to the entrance.

Doug barely seemed to hear.

"Are you buying this?" Bess whispered when they were out of earshot.

Jarli shrugged. "I don't see a reason for him to lie."

"You never see a reason to lie," Bess said. Jarli's bluntness sometimes got him into trouble. "If he's telling the truth, then where are his parents? They've had plenty of time to come here."

"Maybe they did," Jarli said. "Maybe they ate the food while they were waiting . . . and then Viper found them."

They both looked back at Doug, hunched and dirty in the underpass. He did look like an orphan.

"How about we look for the pilot?" Jarli suggested.

Bess's eyebrows shot up. "The pilot who tried to kill Doug?"

"Exactly. If she was working for Viper, she might know his real name or what he looks like. We could follow her. See where she goes, who she meets."

"How would we even find her?"

"I know what she looks like," Jarli said. "I saw her on TV. And I know where her parachute was. Plus I have an app that I think will help."

"No offense, but your apps sometimes do more harm than good."

"We could listen to any calls she makes," Jarli pressed. "In fact, we could steal her phone and give it to the police."

"If Doug's right, Viper's monitoring police communications."

"A private investigator, then." Jarli doubted there was

one in Kelton, but maybe an out-of-towner could do the job. "They could use the pilot's call log and message history to identify Viper publicly. Doug gets to go home to whatever city he came from. Boom. Done."

"Surely the pilot would have deleted anything incriminating," Bess said.

"There are always traces. It's hard to delete stuff off a phone permanently."

"You remember that Doug's a jerk, right? It's not your job to help him."

It's not about who he is, Jarli thought. *It's about who I am.*

Take Cover

A n hour later, Jarli and Doug were both on the bike, bumping down a dirt road toward the parachute. They couldn't afford to wait for daylight. Every second let the pilot get farther away.

Convincing Doug hadn't been as hard as Jarli expected. Spending the night in a freezing underpass must not have appealed to him much. Not that hiking through the bush in the dark was much better.

Bess couldn't come with them. Her crutches would make a hard job impossible. So they had dropped her off at her place on the way. Her job was to track down a private investigator who could help them.

Jarli sent a text to Mum.

Bess says thanks for the lasagna! Delicious. Spending the night at her place.

He couldn't tell her the truth. She wouldn't want him wandering around at night, especially not with Doug. Jarli was pretty sure she wouldn't suspect anything, but he could feel the net of lies tightening around him anyway.

The wind blustered against Jarli's face. Kelton whooshed past, as still and quiet as a cemetery. The full moon looked down on them like a spotlight, somehow making the rest of the world darker. It was like being in a play—the stage lights making the seats invisible. Jarli had turned his phone back on and strapped it to the handlebars so he could use it as a headlight and a GPS.

"You must miss your friends from your old school," he said.

"Yeah," Doug said.

Jarli's phone beeped. *Lie.*

Doug groaned. "That stupid app."

"You *don't* miss your friends?" Jarli asked, surprised.

"I only really had one friend, okay?" Doug said. "And we didn't go to the same school. Everyone in my class hated me. I don't know why. They made fun of me when I got good grades, then they made fun of me when I did badly. The teachers tried to help and only made it worse. Moving to Kelton was lousy, but at least it got me out of that school."

"Sorry," Jarli said.

Doug just grunted.

They didn't talk after that. Not until they reached the tree.

Jarli stared up at it.

"The parachute's gone," he said.

Doug followed his gaze. "You sure this is the right tree?"

"Yeah." Jarli looked around. "Pretty sure."

Doug's phone beeped. *Lie.*

"After all your whining," Jarli said, "you're using my app too?"

"I'm not using your app—I'm using *Truth Premium.*"

"That's even worse," Jarli grumbled. "You've given money to whoever stole my idea."

"Either way—you're *not* sure this is the right tree."

"Not yet. Why did you turn your phone back on?"

"In case we die," Doug said. "Someone can follow the signal and find our bodies. I don't want my parents waiting in an underpass for the rest of their lives, wondering if I'll ever show up."

Jarli couldn't tell if he was kidding. "Great." He pulled his phone off the handlebars, and they trampled across the grass toward the tree. When they got there, he brought up his camera app, and switched it to infrared mode.

On the screen, the world became a swirling mass of colors. Doug was a white blob surrounded by a quivering halo of red and yellow. The trees and dirt were a mixture of blue and black.

"What's that?" Doug asked.

"Infrared," Jarli said. "Most new phones have it built into the camera so they can estimate distances. It's used for augmented reality apps. But it's also handy for detecting heat."

He panned the phone across the dense bush behind them. All cold.

"I was hoping I'd be able to see the pilot's footprints," he muttered, "or the places where she touched the trees. But it's been too long. The trail's gone cold."

"So what do we do?" Doug asked.

"We use another part of the spectrum." Jarli swiped to a different filter, and the landscape on the screen changed color. "Now it's showing static electricity instead of heat. Look!"

The tree where he thought the parachute had been looked fuzzy. The nylon must have rubbed against the branches, leaving a static charge.

"It's the right tree," Jarli said.

Doug looked impressed. "So where's the parachute gone?"

"I told the cops it was here. They must have taken it." Jarli pointed to an animal trail, which sparkled with static. The pilot's uniform must be made of synthetic fibers too. "The pilot went this way. Come on."

As they pushed through the scrub, the hairs on Jarli's arms stood up in the cold, dry air.

"You said the plane had one passenger," Doug said. Jarli had told him this on the way.

"The police thought so, yeah."

"How do we know we're not following the passenger's trail, rather than the pilot's?"

"If the pilot crashed into your house deliberately, it makes sense for her to hide in the bush," Jarli said. "A passenger wouldn't do that. They'd go to the cops."

"But they haven't, right? Do you think they died in the crash?"

"I don't know. Maybe." Jarli hadn't seen a body in the plane, but it was possible that the fire had cremated it. He didn't want to think about that.

He had to keep glancing down at the phone screen as they walked, which meant his eyes couldn't adjust to the darkness. The bush was like a wall of blackness. The foliage above him blocked out the moon. Branches kept coming out of nowhere, scratching his hands and his face.

"How are we going to steal the pilot's phone?" Doug whispered.

"Maybe we won't have to. Maybe we'll overhear her calling somebody. We can record the conversation."

"How will that help?"

Jarli shrugged. "I dunno. Maybe she'll say, 'Hello, Viper. Yes, I know your real name is Joe Shmoe. Yes, I crashed the plane into the house just like you told me to. No, the police don't suspect a thing.'"

"That seems . . . unlikely."

"Well, I'm an optimist."

They kept stumbling through the bush. Jarli tried to move quietly, but the darkness made it hard. Dry twigs crunched underfoot. Leaves rattled around his ankles. Even his breaths felt loud.

There was a bright patch up ahead—as bright on the

screen as Doug or Jarli himself. Jarli swiped back to infrared, and the shape clarified. It was a woman, lying in the leaf litter, perfectly still.

Jarli pointed silently at the glowing blob on the screen. Doug's eyes widened.

He looked like he was thinking the same thing as Jarli. Maybe the pilot had been injured during the crash. She had made it this far into the bush before she collapsed. Now she was unconscious, or dead.

"Maybe she's just sleeping," Jarli whispered. But that sounded like the kind of thing a parent would tell a little kid after spotting a dead kangaroo on the side of the highway. No one would just lie down and sleep in the middle of this cold, scary place.

Their plan was useless now. They couldn't film this person doing anything criminal, and it would feel wrong to steal her phone. In fact, they should probably try to help her. But would Doug be willing to help the woman who destroyed his house?

Doug spoke first. "We have to check," he whispered. "If she's okay."

Jarli nodded, relieved. He and Doug might have more in common than he had thought.

They crept toward the figure on the ground. It was too dark to see her in real life, but the neon shape on the screen was getting bigger and bigger.

Soon Jarli had to stop, because he still couldn't see properly and he was afraid of tripping over the woman. According to the phone, she was right under his feet.

The brightness of the screen made it hard to see anything else. Jarli turned the phone around, shining the light on the shrubbery around his feet.

"Where is she?" Doug whispered.

"She's here somewhere," Jarli replied. The person-shaped blob on the screen was right here. He bent down and reached into the undergrowth. Thanks to the darkness and the thick vegetation, it was an excellent hiding place.

The words "hiding place" caught in Jarli's brain, like a cardigan snagging a nail.

A hand shot out of the undergrowth and grabbed his arm.

"Get down, you idiot!" a voice hissed, and a strong hand dragged Jarli onto the ground.

There was a flash in the distance.

A gunshot rang out.

Doug hit the dirt with a *thump*.

PART TWO
FUGITIVES

I programmed the app to be slightly suspicious of phrases like "and then" or "after that." Liars start at the beginning and finish at the end. People telling the truth jump around all over the place.

—*Documentation from* Truth, *version 2.2*

Black Box

Six Hours Earlier

C abin crew, prepare for landing," Priya Lekis said.

In fact, there was no cabin crew today. No passengers listening to her announcements. No copilot sitting next to her, double-checking everything she did. She'd done this so many times that the words came out anyway. Her plane wasn't on autopilot, but her mouth was.

Her hands fluttered over the controls. Adjusting the flight path here, the altitude there. The engines droned in her ears, muffled by the headphones. She felt the fluid moving in her skull as the pressure changed, reminding her that this wasn't a simulation—she had to do simulated flights each year to keep her license.

Kelton was on the horizon. She'd never been there before. Landing at an unfamiliar airport always put her on edge. The flight simulator didn't even have Kelton programmed in.

Priya was being extra careful, and not just because she didn't have a copilot. Today, without passengers or luggage, the plane was light. The wind kept nudging the nose back and forth.

She still found it ridiculous to be flying an empty plane. According to the accounts department, all the seats had been sold—to a single passenger. The passenger, Steven Fussell, had checked in on his phone. But he hadn't turned up at the airport.

"You have to take off," the ground crew chief had told Priya.

"You're kidding," she'd replied. "There's only one passenger. We're not going to wait for him?"

"He's the only passenger on *this* flight, but not on the next one," the chief said. "They need the plane at the other airport. They don't need a flight crew or a pilot, but they need that plane. You have to go."

"All right. What a waste of fuel."

Before she took off, she hadn't even bothered to close the cockpit door. Now she kept glancing anxiously over her shoulder at all the empty seats behind her. It was weird. She kept imagining faint voices. Like she was flying a plane full of ghosts.

To be fair to the chief, this journey hadn't used much fuel. She was looking at the readings now. She'd started with a whole tank, and it was still two-thirds full. It didn't take much power to keep an empty plane in the air. But still. What kind of weirdo bought every seat on a plane and then didn't turn up to claim any of them?

"Too much money," Priya muttered, before she remembered that the flight recorder—the so-called black box—was listening.

Better not crash, she thought wryly. *They'll hear me being unprofessional.*

Then all the lights in the cockpit went dark.

She didn't panic right away. Sometimes the lights flickered. It had scared her in flight school, but not now. They always came back on.

She waited a second. Two seconds. Three. The lights stayed off. Her heart beat faster and faster as she checked the navigation: dead. Weather readout: dead. Landing gear: dead.

The droning of the engines dropped in pitch and faded away to nothing. Now she was just gliding, with no power. And this was a six-thousand-kilogram tube of steel. It wouldn't stay in the air forever. The nose was already starting to dip.

Priya: dead.

She pushed a button on her radio and tried to sound calm. "Emergency, emergency. This is Priya Lekis, captain of flight DA115. Come in, over."

There was no response.

She tried again: "Emergency! I am experiencing catastrophic power failure on flight DA115. Come in!"

Not even a crackle. Radio: dead.

She pulled her phone out of her pocket. It wouldn't switch on. Whatever had killed the plane seemed to have killed the phone as well. Some kind of freak electrical storm, maybe?

Without the readouts, she couldn't tell exactly how far down the ground was. But before everything went dark, it had been just over ten thousand feet. That meant she had less than five minutes to land this thing.

Feeling sick, she fiddled with the controls. She couldn't control the air brakes or the rudder. She couldn't bring the engines back to life. No way to slow down or change direction. She was going to hit the ground at seven hundred kilometers per hour. *Game over*, as her grizzled old instructor would have said.

She'd done engine failure and emergency landings in the simulator, but not a complete power blackout. This was supposed to be impossible. There were backups. There were backups of those backups.

Priya scrambled out of her seat and lifted a trapdoor behind her. Noise flooded the cockpit. Underneath the trapdoor was a set of cranks and pulleys, shuddering in the shadows.

Those cranks controlled the rudder, the airbrakes, and the landing gear. Priya's instructor had learned in the days when flying was dangerous, and he'd had to use the manual controls once. "It was a bumpy landing," he'd told her, "but it was a landing."

Priya peered through the windscreen. There was a highway to the left of Kelton. Long enough and straight enough. Not too much traffic. She bent down and wound one of the cranks around and around, trying to steer the plane toward the highway.

After thirty seconds of winding the stiff crank, her arm was burning. Sweat poured into her eyes.

She stood up to check her progress.

The plane hadn't changed direction at all. She was still headed straight for Kelton. A small town, but a town nonetheless, with a school, a hospital, a shopping district. If she crashed there, people would die.

She reached back into the trapdoor and kept winding the crank. The floor was sloping now. This glide was becoming more and more like a fall.

Priya stood up again, trying to see how much the aircraft had turned.

Not at all. Kelton was dead ahead, no more than two thousand feet below. And she saw something weird—a light. A single sharp spark, bright enough to hurt Priya's eyes. It was midafternoon, so the only other lights in the town were traffic lights. This wasn't a traffic light. It was too bright, too blue.

The plane was headed straight for it.

Priya had heard rumors of a laser weapon designed to bamboozle aircraft navigation systems. It was like the bogeyman—a story pilots told one another to scare the newbies. But maybe it was true. Perhaps the plane hadn't just malfunctioned. Maybe it had been hijacked remotely.

Priya tried some of the other cranks. Air brakes. Landing gear. Nothing worked. It was as though something had glued all the metal parts of the plane together. None of the important bits would move.

She was going to have to bail out.

The thought terrified her. Skydiving was a risky sport, and unplanned parachute jumps had a miserable survival rate. The closer to the ground she got, the more dangerous it would be, because the parachute needed time to slow her down. A jump from below a hundred feet was almost always fatal.

Priya ran to the equipment locker and wrenched it open. Parachute packs were stacked inside. She'd never used one before, but it was supposed to be idiotproof.

She talked to her radio as she put on the pack, just in case someone could hear her. "Emergency, emergency. This is Priya Lekis, captain of flight DA115. I have lost control of the aircraft. I suspect it has been remotely hijacked. I have no choice but to evacuate. If anyone can hear me, please evacuate the path in front of the aircraft. I repeat, evacuate the path in front of the aircraft." She swallowed. "Or shoot the plane down, if you have to."

She tightened the straps over her chest and ran for the emergency exit. Her hand hesitated over the bright red handle. All pilots were terrified of cabin depressurization. Even a small hole in the hull could suck all the oxygen out of the aircraft. After eight seconds, passengers would be too confused to put on their oxygen masks. Within fifteen seconds they'd be unconscious. Four minutes until total brain death. *Game over.*

Priya told herself that the plane was too close to the ground for the oxygen to be sucked out. Cabin pressure was not an issue. She took one last hopeful glance toward the controls— still dark. Then she sucked in a deep breath and pulled the handle.

There was a scream as the seal broke around the edges of the emergency exit. It was deafening, even through her headphones. The rushing wind turned the plane into the world's largest flute. Priya wrenched the whole door inward, twisted it, and then hurled it out into the daylight. It was immediately sucked away.

Priya peered through the gap, squinting against the wind. She was both too high and too low for comfort. But the longer she waited, the more dangerous the jump would be.

She leaped out of the plane.

A wall of air hit Priya, sending her spinning. The sun and the ground swapped places, over and over. The wing of the plane whooshed past overhead, so close that it pulled her into its wake for a moment. Then the plane was gone, and it was just Priya, alone in the sky with the thundering wind.

No time to lose. She needed to rip open the pouch on the side of the pack, but her freezing fingers were shaky and numb. The trees below grew and grew. Landing on grass would be okay. Water was bad. Trees were death.

She finally managed to tear the pouch open and grab the drogue inside. She pulled it out and let go.

Nothing happened.

Priya screamed as she hurtled toward the ground—

With a tremendous *ZZZZIP*, the parachute slithered out of the pack above her. The wind filled it up, and the nylon ropes went taut. All the straps jerked tight over Priya's chest, bruising her ribs and pushing all the air out of her. It felt like hitting a wall.

But she didn't stop. She was still falling, alarmingly fast.

There was a road nearby. Paddocks on one side, trees on the other. Even landing on the asphalt would be better than hitting those trees. She yanked on the ropes, trying to steer herself toward it.

The chute tilted, but not enough. Her kicking feet were still over the deadly branches.

"Come on!" she yelled, tugging harder.

BOOM! There was a bright flash as the plane hit the ground on the horizon. Priya felt like she was going to throw up. What had it landed on? How many people had been hurt?

She had almost reached the road. She braced herself for impact—

But it never came. The chute snagged a tree next to the road. She swung back toward the trunk, covering her face just in time.

WHAM! She hit the tree, arms first. Something snapped in her shoulder, and pain flooded up her neck. She recognized the sensation from a childhood fall—her collarbone had snapped. She had kept the X-ray under her bed for years, a source of quiet pride.

Priya dangled there on the creaking nylon ropes, helpless. But alive.

She looked around. She couldn't believe it. A total power failure during a flight was unlikely, and surviving it was even more unlikely. Just wait until her instructor heard about this.

As she finally pulled her headphones off her sweaty ears, she heard engine noise. Distant, but coming closer. Someone could already be coming to pick her up.

Priya grabbed a branch with one hand and balanced her feet on another. She started unbuckling the straps across her chest.

Then she wondered why there were no sirens.

If emergency services were coming to get her, they would have their sirens on. In fact, they would probably be heading for the crash site, not for her.

So who was coming?

She held a hand over her eyes, shielding them from the sun. Two black vans were on the horizon, breaking the speed limit as they hurtled up the highway toward her. Not police.

They could be random motorists. But was that likely, all the way out here?

Or—and this was what really worried her—they might be the owners of the bright light.

The ones who had crashed the plane.

Taking Fire

Doug!" Jarli cried.

"I'm okay," Doug said. He hadn't been hit by the gunshot—he had just thrown himself to the ground.

"Quiet, both of you!" the pilot hissed.

There was another shot. The bullet hit a nearby tree with a *thwack*, showering the ground with bark.

"Someone's shooting at us!" Jarli said, still reeling from the shock.

"Quiet!" the pilot snapped.

Now that Jarli was lying next to the woman, he could see that her pilot's uniform was ripped. A bruise had swollen her eye almost shut. She didn't look like someone who had crashed a plane on purpose.

"They know where we are now," she whispered. "We have to move."

"Who are they?"

"I think they crashed my plane. They've been looking for me. There are two of them, maybe more. Listen."

Jarli did. The wind moaned. Frogs croaked. There were no voices and no more gunshots.

After a long pause, Doug said, "Maybe they're gone."

"Shhh," the pilot said. "They're not gone. They're waiting for us to make a move."

Doug looked around. "Where are they?"

"I don't know."

Jarli was so scared that his teeth were chattering. He tried to work out where the gunshots had come from. But they had been so sudden, and the thick forest had muffled and distorted the sound of the weapons firing.

"On the count of three, we run," the pilot said. "Uphill. We don't want them to have the higher ground. Got it?"

Doug nodded. His face was white.

"One," the pilot whispered. "Two—"

"Wait!" Jarli hissed. "Stop."

"What?"

Jarli felt around the dirt until he found a rock. He scooped it up. "We can distract them."

The pilot quickly saw what he meant. "I can't throw it," she said. "My collarbone is broken."

"I'll do it," Jarli said. Very, very slowly, he rose into a crouch. Looking through the trees, he still couldn't see the shooter. It was impossible not to imagine someone training their sights on him right now. His heart was going at a million miles an hour. He wondered if he would feel the bullet, or if he would be dead before he knew what happened.

He took a deep breath and flung the rock as hard as he could. The swing jarred his shoulder. The rock struck a distant tree trunk way downhill and then crashed into the shrubbery around it, spilling echoes through the bush.

Almost immediately, Jarli heard boots crashing through the undergrowth somewhere to his left. The bad guys had heard the distraction. Now they were sprinting toward the spot where the rock had landed.

Jarli dropped to the ground.

"Go, go!" the pilot hissed.

They crawled through the undergrowth as quickly and quietly as geckos, occasionally pausing to listen. Even with one arm hanging limp, the pilot moved fast. Jarli struggled to keep up, his jaw clenched, his muscles tense. Every movement he made felt too loud. At least it was easier to crawl uphill than it would have been to crawl down, headfirst.

He couldn't hear the boots anymore. He wondered when the shooters would realize they had been tricked.

"There!" a voice yelled.

A bullet whizzed out of the darkness and thunked into a tree just above Jarli's head.

"Run!" Jarli whispered.

The others scrambled to their feet as another gunshot rang out. Jarli raced after them, arms swinging, feet thumping the dirt. The second shot seemed to come from a different angle. The bad guys had split up. Now they were moving in from different directions to trap the pilot and the two kids.

"Look!" Doug pointed to a spot of deep darkness higher up the hillside. It looked like the entrance to a cave.

But it was at least thirty meters away, and there was no cover. The bad guys would have a clear shot.

"They won't find us in there," Doug said.

The pilot took cover next to Doug, half-hidden behind a rock about the size of a suitcase. "It's too far," she whispered. "We won't make it!"

"We can't stay here," Doug insisted.

The boots crashed through the scrub, moving closer and closer to them.

"Freeze!" someone yelled.

Jarli covered his head with his arms. This was the end.

Then he recognized the voice. It was Constable Frink.

"It's the cops!" one of the bad guys hissed. Their footsteps changed direction.

"Stop! Police!" another voice said. It sounded like Constable Blanco.

"I don't see them," Frink said. "Split up. You go that way."

"Over here!" the pilot yelled.

Doug shushed her. "No police!"

"*What?* Why?"

Jarli hesitated. Doug thought Viper was monitoring police

communications because, before the crash, only the police had known who Doug and his parents really were. If Jarli got the attention of Blanco and Frink, he could warn them that Viper was spying on them. But two men with guns were hiding somewhere in the darkness. Was it too risky to call out?

Now it was too late. The yelling and footsteps were getting farther and farther away.

"Who are you?" the pilot asked. "What are you doing here?"

"Let's get out of sight," Doug said. "Before they come back."

The Fear Scale

When they got to the cave, Priya Lekis told Jarli and Doug the whole story—the mysterious passenger who bought every seat and then didn't show up, the sudden blackout in the cockpit, the last-second parachute jump that saved her life.

Jarli shivered. The cave was as cold, dark, and damp as the underpass had been, and it was cramped with the three of them huddled inside. Jarli didn't like enclosed spaces. The last time Viper came after him, Jarli had survived by hiding in one of the old mining tunnels beneath Kelton. Sometimes he had nightmares about it—crouching in the dark, too scared to go any deeper into the tunnel, but unable to climb out because of the fire raging above.

Now it seemed like they were back to square one. If the pilot wasn't part of Viper's plan, she couldn't help them unmask him.

Then Priya mentioned the weird light down in Kelton drawing the plane toward it.

"Magnetic laser," Jarli whispered.

Priya looked puzzled. "What?"

Doug's eyes widened. "You think that's how Viper crashed the plane? With the device he bought from Magnotech?"

Jarli thought of the guys at the crash site with their metal detectors, and the strange object he had seen them pick up. The thing which had looked a bit like a data projector.

Could that have been the magnetic device? Viper must have used it to yank the plane right down onto Doug's house. Then he sent his two goons to recover it from the wreckage.

"Who or what is Viper?" Priya asked.

"A criminal," Doug said. "About a year ago he purchased an experimental magnetic laser. And today your plane crashed into . . . into the house of one of his enemies. A witness who was providing evidence against him. We know about Viper because he almost killed Jarli once before."

Jarli clenched his fists, fighting back visions of the car crash. The morgue. The fire.

Priya looked from Jarli to Doug and back again.

"You're not messing with me?" she asked.

Jarli swallowed. "It's all true."

"And you can trust him," Doug added. "He's the guy who invented the *Truth* app."

Priya blinked. "Huh. Really? I have that on my phone— well, the premium version."

Jarli sighed.

"But my phone got fried," the pilot continued.

"At the same time as the plane went dark?" Doug asked.

"Right. At the time I thought it might have been an electrical storm."

"Is it even possible to make a magnet strong enough to knock out a plane and bring it down on a specific spot?" Jarli asked.

"If it is," Priya said slowly, "every terrorist group in the world would want one. Probably every military force too. No government likes having its airspace invaded."

"Viper could name his price," Doug said. "Now that he's proven that the device works. All this news coverage is like free advertising."

Jarli tried to imagine a world in which any plane could be shot out of the sky at any time by a magnetic beam from below. *No one would fly anywhere*, he thought. On the fear scale, plane crashes were right up there with shark attacks. But train and ferry companies would make a lot of money. Maybe Viper owned one.

"It can't be a coincidence that one person bought every seat on the plane," Doug said slowly.

"You think Viper was trying to kill the passenger?" Jarli asked. "Not just your . . . the witness?"

"Maybe the passenger found out that Viper was going to attack the plane, and that was why he didn't get on board," Doug said. "Priya, do you remember his name?"

"Well, the ground crew paged him a bunch of times: *This is an urgent page for Mr. . . .*" Priya closed her eyes. "Steven Fussell. That was it."

"It's a clue," Jarli said. "Something the police could use."

"Except we can't tell them," Doug said.

"You're seriously not going to the police?" Priya looked incredulous. "You're kids. You can't investigate this yourselves. We have to contact the authorities."

"The person whose house got destroyed," Doug said, "was in witness protection. Only the police knew where she was, and Viper found out. Did we mention that you're a wanted criminal?"

"I'm what?"

"The cops think you crashed the plane deliberately. If you turn yourself in, do you think you'll have a chance to convince them you're innocent before Viper gets you?"

Priya put her face in her hands. "This is a nightmare. I just want to go home."

"Me too," Doug said. "But I can't." He turned to Jarli. "You can, though. The bad guys don't know who you are yet. If you don't turn up at school tomorrow, or do anything else suspicious—"

Jarli's phone was ringing. "Hang on." He checked the screen. Bess was calling.

He answered. "Hey, Bess. What's going on?"

"I have some bad news and some good news," Bess said.

"Bad news first," Jarli said. That was always his policy.

"There are no private investigators in Kelton. And no one from out of town will come here at a price we can afford."

"What's the good news?"

"I found a phone number for someone else who I'm sure will help us."

Jarli was too doubtful to feel relieved. "Is it someone who has money, connections, and investigation experience who isn't with the police but also isn't a criminal? And who won't charge us?"

"Yep. But you're not going to like it."

"Try me," Jarli said.

On Camera

S MASH! The door burst off its hinges. The impact nearly collapsed the wall around it too. The house had seen
better days.

The battering ram clanged against the concrete porch as
police officers swarmed into the house, bulked up by bullet-
proof vests and helmets.

Someone inside started swearing. His voice carried
through the broken windows.

"Police!" someone else yelled. "Get on the floor, facedown.
Do it now!"

Dana Reynolds was hiding behind an unmarked van on
the other side of the street. Her camera operator and her
producer huddled next to her. Reynolds rehearsed her lines
in her head. *When Henry Pollick bought this house three
years ago, neighbors soon noticed that he wasn't much of a
groundskeeper.*

"Now," the producer said.

Reynolds moved across the street as fast as she could without ruining her hair. She inhaled deeply as she walked up the

cracked path toward the front door. She didn't want to sound out of breath.

As soon as the police were out of the way, she stepped onto the porch and turned to face the camera. The spotlight was bright. She fought the urge to squint as she held the microphone in front of her chin.

"When Henry Pollick bought this house three years ago," she began, "neighbors soon noticed that he wasn't much of a groundskeeper. Weeds overtook the path. Leaves blocked the gutters. But none of them suspected they were living next door . . . to a criminal."

She kept her face severe, chin up, one eyebrow slightly raised. She called this expression The Vice Principal.

"Police are searching the building behind me," she said. "They hope to find almost two hundred thousand dollars stolen from three banks around Kelton over the past six months. But there are fears that the money may already have been spent."

Reynolds stepped aside just as the police dragged Pollick out of the house. He was wearing boxer shorts and a tattered black T-shirt that barely covered his skinny arms. His gray hair was matted on one side—he'd been pulled out of bed. His hands were already cuffed behind his back.

As usual, the police didn't look happy to see Reynolds and her news crew. But they were smart enough to keep quiet on camera.

Pollick wasn't.

"I've been framed!" he bellowed, showering the producer with spit. "This is a stitch-up!"

Holding him by his upper arms, two police officers hauled him up the path toward the waiting paddy wagon.

Reynolds waited for the camera to turn back to her. "Sources have confirmed that charges will be laid tonight," she continued, "and the trial will begin within a month. I'm Dana Reynolds, and this is *Nationwide*."

She kept looking at the camera until the producer gave her a thumbs-up.

Reynolds let the air out of her lungs and stretched her neck. The beds in the Kelton motel were subpar, but the network wouldn't pay for a room at the golf resort west of town. She needed *sleep*. Why couldn't the police catch bank robbers at sensible times of day?

Hopefully they would solve the plane crash mystery soon. Then Reynolds could file her story and go back home to Swancliff.

"Any cursing?" she asked.

"Only while he was still in the house," the producer said, wiping her glasses. "We can bleep it. Nothing while you were talking."

The paddy wagon drove away with Pollick and two police officers inside. Two more officers stayed behind. Reynolds recognized them—there weren't many cops in Kelton. Their names were Blanco and Frink. Both looked sweaty and disheveled, with dirty shoes. *Interesting,* Reynolds thought. *Where have they been?*

As soon as the paddy wagon was gone, the operator lowered his camera. The producer switched her phone back on, and it immediately started ringing. Blanco and Frink approached.

"Dana Reynolds," Blanco said. "Shouldn't you be out ruining someone's life?"

"Demonizing a local religious group, maybe?" Frink suggested.

"Or giving airtime to a crackpot?"

"Blaming cops for the crime rate instead of criminals?"

"Shouldn't *you* be looking for that criminal who escaped from your jail?" Reynolds shot back. "Cobra has been at large for months now—care to comment?"

Blanco scowled. "That's a federal case now."

Reynolds turned to Frink. "You were federal until recently, right? What have you heard from your old colleagues?"

Frink said, "We don't discuss leads—"

"In an active investigation. Blah, blah." Reynolds checked her watch. "Are either of you two clowns going to make an official statement about Pollick, or can I get back to work?"

"Are you going to tell us how you knew about this secret predawn raid?" Blanco asked.

"No comment," Reynolds said. First law of journalism: Protect your sources.

"Then that's a 'no comment' from us, too."

"Good talk." Reynolds turned back to her camera operator. "Get some more footage around the back of the house. Peeling paint, broken roof tiles, whatever you can find."

With a parting glare, the cops disappeared. The camera operator trudged through the overgrown yard.

"Where's my coffee?" Reynolds demanded.

The producer held out a phone.

Reynolds glared at her. "That's not coffee."

"Jarli Durras is on the phone."

"The *Truth*-app kid? He's old news."

"He claims he witnessed the plane crash yesterday afternoon and was the first to run into the wreckage. He's willing to do a face-to-face."

That did sound like a good story, but if Reynolds remembered correctly, Jarli had always avoided the media. Why was he suddenly happy to be on TV?

"Did he say what he wants in return?"

The producer shook her head. "Maybe he has a new app to plug."

Reynolds sighed. Probably. She pulled out her earpiece, then took the phone and unmuted it.

"Jarli!" she said, with as much cheer as she could muster this early in the morning. "Thanks for reaching out. How are you?"

The boy's voice sounded shaky. "I've been trying to get through to you for hours."

"Sorry," Reynolds said. "Working on a big story. I gather you were at the scene of the accident today? Wow. That must have been terrifying."

This conversation wasn't being recorded, so Reynolds could turn the charm up to eleven. Everyone got the charm off camera. Most of them got it on camera, too—except cops, politicians, and alleged criminals.

"Yeah," Jarli said. "Is this a secure line?"

She rolled her eyes. Already, her conspiracy nut alarm was ringing. "Yes. This is the phone I use for confidential sources. No one's listening at my end."

"Okay." Reynolds heard Jarli take a deep breath. "The plane crash wasn't an accident."

Reynolds said nothing. This was an old journo's trick—let the interviewee get uncomfortable and fill the silence.

"There were no passengers on board," Jarli continued. "The plane was hijacked remotely by an electromagnetic device. The hijacker crashed it into that house on purpose, to kill witnesses in a police investigation."

Dana's conspiracy nut alarm was still ringing, but there was something else as well. That tingling in her toes. The sense that a good story was on the horizon.

"I have Priya Lekis here with me," Jarli said. "The pilot everyone's looking for."

"Put her on," Reynolds said.

In Plain Sight

The soccer ball came out of nowhere and hit Jarli in the side of the head. He toppled over like he'd been struck by a meteorite. Other kids were already laughing by the time his face hit the grass.

"Jarli," Mr. Hayes yelled. "What are you doing?"

Jarli rolled over. The sunshine dazzled him. "Headbutting the ball, sir," he groaned. "Just like in the World Cup."

"Well, next time use your forehead." Hayes pulled Jarli to his feet. "You don't want to wind up with a concussion."

His classmates were smirking. Jarli was too tired to care. He had read somewhere that being awake produced toxic proteins that made it hard to think; only sleep could wash them away. He could almost feel the toxins jammed between his brain cells. He would have given anything to go back to bed. Lunch break started in ten minutes. Maybe he could sneak into the library for a nap in one of the beanbags.

He couldn't go home. The bad guys knew his face, but they didn't know his name. When Dana Reynolds had realized he was serious and ditched the fake-nice voice, she had said that Doug and the pilot should stay hidden, but Jarli and Bess should act like everything was normal. Viper might be looking for kids who didn't turn up to school today.

Also, Jarli still didn't want to get his parents involved.

Reynolds and her team were trying to find Steven Fussell, the passenger who hadn't boarded the flight. They were also trying to learn more about the magnetic device Viper might have used. Meanwhile, Jarli was at school, pretending everything was fine.

His act wasn't fooling everyone. Anya ran over. She stopped next to Jarli, under the pretext of a hamstring stretch.

"Jarli," she said quietly. "Are you okay?"

Anya was the quiet, watchful daughter of Russian immigrants. Her main sport was boxing, but she seemed equally good at soccer—she'd scored two of the three goals in this game so far. Last time Viper had come after Jarli, Anya had been a huge help. Jarli trusted her.

"The ball didn't hit me that hard," he replied.

"I do not mean the ball," Anya said. "You have been acting strangely all morning."

Jarli looked around. He kept his voice low. "I can't talk about it."

Anya nodded slowly. "Can I help?"

"Thanks, but I don't think so."

"Well, let me know if you change your mind." Anya shifted her gaze, looking over Jarli's shoulder. "Bess wants something." Then she ran off after the ball.

Jarli turned. Bess was sitting by the sidelines, waving like a devoted mum. Her crutches lay on the grass beside her.

What? Jarli mouthed.

Bess pointed at the fence.

The ball rolled past Jarli. He realized a moment later that he probably should have kicked it.

"Wake up, Jarli," someone shouted.

Yeah, he thought. *Wake up, Jarli.* Revealing how tired he was could be just as bad as not turning up.

He tried to jog after the crowd of kids surrounding the ball, but he lost his footing almost immediately. The collision with his head had left him dizzy, or maybe it was just exhaustion.

"Jarli," Hayes said. "You okay?"

Jarli looked up to reassure Hayes that he was fine. Then he saw what Bess had been pointing at through the fence. A police van had pulled up near the school. Two men in dark suits and sunglasses were climbing out. One was bald. The other had curly brown hair. They looked like funeral directors, except maybe younger and fitter. Probably Federal Police, since the van had a government license plate.

The driver took off his sunnies, revealing dark circles around his eyes. Jarli recognized him. He had been one of the men in hazmat suits. The one with the metal detector—Scanner.

The realization hit Jarli like a blow to the chest. Doug had thought Viper was intercepting police communications. But the truth was even worse: Viper had a cop working for him.

The other man was bald. Last night, Jarli hadn't seen the second hazmat man's face, but he had seen his blond hair. So this was someone else.

The two men walked toward the front of the school, out of sight.

"Jarli," Hayes said again. He looked worried. "Can you hear me?"

"What? Yeah."

"I think you'd better go to the nurse."

"I'm not sick," Jarli said. *Act normal.*

But this was the wrong thing to say. Hayes was always suspicious of kids who claimed to be sick or injured. He was alarmed when they claimed not to be.

"Go," he said. "Let Nurse Eaton have a look at you."

Bess was hobbling over. "I'll take him."

Hayes nodded. "Good idea. Make sure he doesn't get lost."

"Those guys are cops," Bess whispered, as they hurried across the oval toward the gym. "Feds."

"I know," Jarli muttered.

"And one of them was at the crash site last night."

"I know."

"What are we gonna do?"

"Act normal, I guess," Jarli said. "They don't know who we are."

"They know what we look like," Bess said. "Especially me." She was the only girl at the school who used crutches to get around.

"Then we need somewhere to hide. I guess the nurse's office will have to do."

Nurse Maria Eaton shone a painfully bright light in Jarli's face. His eyes watered. He wondered idly if he would look more honest now that she had basically blinded him. He had programmed his app to check pupil size, since thinking of a lie tended to make pupils briefly dilate.

"You remember your name?" Eaton asked.

"Jarli Durras."

"You know what day it is?"

"Tuesday."

Eaton switched off the light. She scribbled some notes on Jarli's patient file, rolled her computer chair over to a chest of drawers, and put the light inside. The office was so cramped that there was barely enough room for the chair to fit between the bed and her desk. There was no daylight. The only window was boarded up, because Jarli had smashed it the last time he was here. He had been trying to escape from Viper's assassin, Cobra. He wondered how the nurse could spend all day in this dark, tiny room without going crazy.

"You're fine," Eaton said. "Was this just an excuse for you two to get out of class?"

Eaton had once been a surgeon in the army. Jarli suspected that anything less than a missing limb counted as "fine."

"No," Bess said. "Mr. Hayes insisted. That ball hit Jarli hard."

"Uh-huh. You feel okay, Jarli?"

"Pretty tired." Jarli looked longingly at the narrow bed. "But I don't think that's a symptom. I stayed up kind of late last night."

"Sounds like cause and effect to me," Eaton said. Jarli had thought nurses were supposed to be gentle, but Eaton was always blunt. Her trust rating on *Truth Premium* was 100 percent.

The phone buzzed on Eaton's desk. She picked it up. "Yes?"

She listened for a moment. Then she looked at Jarli.

"No," she said. "Anything else?"

A pause. Jarli could hear the neon lights humming.

"Okay. Thanks." She hung up.

"What's going on?" Jarli asked.

Eaton hesitated for a moment, as though she wasn't sure how much to tell him. Then she said, "Apparently, someone at reception wanted to know if any students have gone home sick today."

Goose bumps grew on Jarli's arms.

"Who's asking?" he asked.

"The receptionist didn't say. Why?"

Jarli just shrugged. He felt Eaton's eyes on him like a laser.

"You two know something I don't?" she asked.

"Us? No," Jarli said.

"Of course not," Bess added.

Eaton's phone buzzed. *Lie.*

"I made that app," Jarli said. "It's not as reliable as everyone thinks."

The phone buzzed again. *Lie.*

"See?" Bess said.

Eaton sat back down. Her computer chair squeaked. "Okay," she said. "Who's at reception, and what are they looking for?"

Jarli and Bess looked at each other.

"Have you been causing some kind of trouble?" Eaton asked.

"We can't talk about it," Bess said. "But we haven't done anything wrong."

"Next they might ask the receptionist if anyone is still at school but not in class. That will lead them here. I could get another call any minute."

"Why would the school tell them?"

"Why indeed?" Eaton looked Jarli up and down. "They must be someone official. If that's the case, I'll need to tell them what I know."

Eaton's phone rang again. She and Jarli both looked at it.

"Am I going to answer that?" she asked.

"Please, don't," Jarli pleaded. "We're in danger. Some bad people are looking for us."

"It's to do with the plane crash yesterday," Bess added.

"We know some stuff about it, and they don't want anyone else to find out."

Eaton picked up her phone.

Jarli stood up. He and Bess needed to leave.

But the nurse rejected the call and held the phone up to Jarli's face. "Say that again," she said.

Jarli spoke quickly: "Some bad guys are looking for us because we know things about the plane crash yesterday. They'll hurt us if they find us."

Eaton looked at the screen, which flashed green. Jarli wasn't lying.

"Interesting," she said finally. "How much do you know about them?"

"Not much. But—"

Someone knocked on the door.

Secret Tunnel

Jarli felt the blood drain out of his face. Bess's knuckles were white around her crutches.

The knock came again. Louder. And a voice: "Miss Eaton?"

Jarli looked at the boarded-up window. Prying the boards off would be too loud and too slow. They couldn't get out that way.

Eaton made some hand signals at Jarli and Bess. They both shook their heads. Neither of them knew any sign language.

The door handle turned, but the door didn't open. It was locked.

Eaton put a finger to her lips.

Jarli nodded. He knew that sign.

The nurse crouched down and crawled under the bed. Jarli stared. Was her plan to *hide* from the bad guys? If they broke in, under the bed was the first place they would check. And there wasn't room for all three of them under there.

"Maybe the kids have gone back to class already," said a man outside the door.

"Maybe not," another man replied. "We need a key for this door."

There was a faint *clunk* from beneath the bed. Jarli bent down and saw an air vent under there. Eaton had removed the grill, revealing a dark metal tunnel. It looked just big enough to crawl through.

Eaton beckoned to Bess and pointed to the tunnel.

Bess's eyes widened.

Jarli swallowed. The tunnel was very narrow. What if he got stuck?

But those guys sounded like they were coming in soon. And there was no other way out. Bess was already wriggling into the tunnel, one hand holding the crutches out in front. Jarli watched her legs disappear. Eaton gestured for him to go next.

Jarli crawled under the bed and squeezed into the vent. The steel walls pressed against his shoulders, and the ceiling rubbed the back of his head. Every instinct screamed at him to go back.

He went forward instead, wriggling like an earthworm. His body blocked the light from the infirmary. He couldn't see anything other than Bess's dirty shoes up ahead. How long was the vent?

There was a muffled clanking sound from behind him, and he realized that Eaton had crawled into the vent too. Now he really couldn't go back. The thought made it hard to breathe.

A hand grabbed his ankle, and he jolted.

"Stop," Eaton whispered.

Jarli froze. So did Bess.

Keys rattled. A door creaked. The men were in the nurse's office.

Jarli stayed frozen, his heart in his mouth. Eaton's hand was like concrete around his ankle. He hoped she'd closed the grille behind her somehow.

"Not here," one voice said.

"There'll be patient records," the other replied. "You check the computer, I'll try the filing cabinet."

Rustling papers. Tapping keys.

"Password protected."

"Never mind. I found it. Jarli Durras—possible concussion. Here's his address, phone number, treatment history . . ."

"Anything about the girl?"

"Not that I can see."

"Try to phone Durras."

Jarli quickly reached for his phone. It was hard to dig it out of his pocket in the confines of the vent, but he managed it. Unable to see the screen, he held the power button until he felt the phone vibrate and shut down.

"Did you hear something?" one of the voices said, quieter now.

"Yeah. Someone outside, maybe. Let's check it out."

Footsteps scuffled away. The door closed. Silence.

"Okay," Eaton whispered. "Keep moving."

Bess started crawling again. Jarli followed.

Soon they found the other end of the vent. Jarli slithered out and uncoiled his body gratefully.

He couldn't see much in the dark, but the echoes told him that this was a small room with hard surfaces. It smelled ancient and undisturbed, like the cave in the bush last night.

"Where are we?" Bess whispered.

"It's left over from the mining days." As Eaton emerged from the vent, she used her phone screen to cast some light across the room. An old hurricane lamp was mounted on a brick wall between two metal doors. Each door had two big padlocks— one with a combination, the other with a keyhole. The doors looked old and rusted, but the padlocks were shiny and new.

"If you don't want me to report this, I need you to tell me everything," Eaton said. "But first we have to get you as far away from the school as possible."

Jarli was still staring at the doors. "How did you find this place?"

"Rule number two in the army," Eaton said. "Find and protect all access points to home base."

"What was rule number one?" Bess asked.

"Rule one was 'Don't ask questions.'" Eaton was already unlocking one of the doors. She had the key to one padlock and knew the combination to the other. She must have put them there.

"You're not in the army anymore," Jarli said.

"They tell new recruits that the friends you make there will last forever," Eaton said. "Unfortunately, that's also true of enemies."

The door opened with a squawk of old hinges. Beyond was a rectangle of blackness. As Jarli's eyes adjusted, he saw stone walls and a ceiling held up by wooden beams.

"I'll have to show you the way," Eaton said. "If you get lost down here, you'll never find your way out."

Jarli gulped and followed her into the blackness.

Nightmares

Doug woke when a mosquito flew into his ear.

He yelped and slapped himself in the side of the head. It hurt, but the mosquito flew off. He wondered if it had bitten him already. As a kid he had read a book that featured a mosquito as big as a horse, chasing the main character through a forest. The scene had scared him so much that he was still frightened of mosquitos, years later.

Doug sat up, rubbing his eyes. His face and hands were freezing. Birds were chattering and trees were rustling.

He hadn't intended to fall asleep. He'd just been so tired. After Jarli left, Doug and Priya had argued for most of the night—she still wanted to go to the police, and he still thought it was a bad idea. Eventually she had given up. Doug had been sitting down, then leaning on one elbow, then lying down. Priya had said she needed to go to the bathroom and walked outside. Doug had closed his eyes, just for a second. Now suddenly the sun was up.

He'd been dreaming about his old house, from before he'd come to Kelton. In the dream, his parents had been put in witness protection without him. They had changed their names and moved away, leaving him behind in an empty house. He was going through the stuff in their bedroom, searching for clues about what their new names might be, getting more and more frantic. Because Viper was coming, and Doug needed to be gone by the time he arrived.

And then there was a scratching sound at his parents' bedroom door. Viper was already *inside the house—*

And Doug woke up.

He had this nightmare often, but it had been especially vivid this time. It took him a minute to reassure himself that it had only been a dream. Then he turned to ask Priya if he'd missed anything important.

She wasn't there.

Doug looked around. The cave was dark and empty. In the light of day, he could see that it was small, with no tunnels or other openings.

He crept over to the mouth of the cave and peered out. There was no movement among the trees. No sign of Priya's black-and-white pilot uniform.

"Priya," he hissed. His voice was still rough-edged from sleep. "Are you there?"

The bush took his voice and gave nothing back.

He called out louder. "Priya? Where are you?"

Insects hummed. Leaves rustled.

Doug took a deep breath. *The bad guys haven't found her,*

he told himself. *Because they would have taken me, too. So where is she?*

Only one possibility remained. Priya had left. She had gone looking for the police because she trusted them more than some kids and a stranger on the phone who claimed to be a journalist.

Fair enough, Doug had to admit. But now he had a problem. Priya knew where he was. She would tell the cops. Then Viper would find him.

He had to move.

Doug took one last look around the cave to check that he hadn't left any traces behind. Then he trudged out into the trees.

He walked in a random direction, because he wasn't sure what he was looking for, exactly. Maybe another cave. Maybe a trail leading to a disused cabin, or a farm with a barn he could hide in. Maybe he should walk to his family's storage locker—it was on the edge of town, so he wouldn't have to go through Kelton to get there.

He kept his eyes on the ground as he walked. A twisted ankle could be disastrous. *Can't be on the run if you can't run*, he thought.

Even watching the ground, Doug nearly stepped in a ditch that was almost completely hidden by ferns and fallen branches. He was still looking for a way around it when he heard the footsteps up ahead.

Priya. She must have left only minutes before he woke up. This gave him a second chance. If he could catch up with her, he could talk her out of leaving.

"Priya!" he yelled.

The footsteps stopped.

Doug waited for Priya to call back, but she didn't. There was a long silence.

Then the footsteps started again. Getting louder. Closer. They were heavy. Too heavy to be Priya.

Doug jumped down into the ditch. The prickly ferns swallowed him up. He found himself enclosed in green, like a seed in a pod.

He waited.

Blackdamp

A lot of coal miners died down here," Eaton told Jarli and Bess as they walked. "Mine collapses, fires, explosions, suffocations. There was talk of getting a nuclear power plant instead, but then the Chernobyl reactor melted down in Russia. That scared everyone, so they kept mining coal until the late nineties. One big disaster gets more attention than a hundred smaller ones. Just like how a plane crash gets more attention than a hundred car accidents."

Jarli didn't know if she was trying to scare them, or if this was just how army people talked. They were walking downhill, which worried him. Going deeper and deeper underground. He could hear Bess's crutches clacking on the rough stone behind him.

"You know the way out, right?" Bess said.

"I know five ways out. Only two of them are a significant distance from the school, though. I think it's time for you to tell me who's after you."

Jarli was still wondering how much to reveal when Bess spoke up.

"We think they work for a crime lord called Viper," she said. "Have you heard of him?"

There was a pause. Eaton's footsteps echoed through the darkness. Water dripped somewhere in the distance.

"There are rumors," Eaton said finally, "of a man with terrible scars all over his face. Burns, like you get from a bomb blast. People say he's based in Kelton and has criminals working for him all over the country. But I don't believe the rumors are true."

Lie. Jarli's phone beeped. It must have turned itself back on. Could that mean Eaton *did* believe the stories she'd heard?

"Where did you hear these rumors?" he asked.

"I don't appreciate you using that app on me," Eaton said.

"We think Viper brought down the plane," Bess said, "because it crashed into the house of a witness working against him. But we don't know Viper's real name, or anything about his organization."

"It doesn't sound like you're much of a threat to Viper," Eaton said thoughtfully.

Jarli had been thinking the same thing. "But he doesn't know that," he said. "And if we're right, he must have police working for him, because otherwise he wouldn't know where the witness lived. And now the Feds are chasing us."

"Wait. The people we're running from are Federal Police?"

It sounded like Eaton was second-guessing her decision to help them.

"Police who work for a crime boss," Jarli said.

"Jarli found the pilot," Bess said. "She says some kind of laser beam crashed her plane. And we know Viper met with someone from Magnotech about a year ago to order a magnetic laser. We have a journalist trying to find out more."

"Is the pilot okay?" Eaton asked. "Do you have her hidden somewhere safe?"

"Safe-ish," Bess said. "We probably shouldn't tell you where."

"Smart. Watch your head."

Jarli ducked just in time to avoid a low-hanging rock. He wondered how many miners had been injured by it.

"Can you trust this journalist?" Eaton asked. "Who is it?"

"Dana Reynolds," Jarli said cautiously. "Why wouldn't we trust her?"

"Well, she's not helping you out of the goodness of her heart." Eaton hesitated at a fork in the tunnel and then turned left. Jarli followed, hoping she wasn't lost.

"You think she might work for Viper?" Bess asked.

"Probably not," Eaton said. "But even if her goals line up with yours, Viper might get to her. Then she might decide to sacrifice you to save herself."

Jarli felt like he was descending too fast in an elevator.

"You think we should have gone to the police instead?"

"You have no way of knowing which cops can be trusted. So no. You're in a tight spot. If I were you, I wouldn't trust anybody. That's rule number five."

It was hard to tell, but Jarli thought Eaton sounded sad. Jarli wondered what sort of person only felt safe if her office had a locked door and a secret tunnel. Maybe her trust rating was so high because she almost never had anyone to talk to.

"Sounds like a lonely way to live," Bess said, echoing Jarli's thoughts.

"Yes," Eaton said. "But you'll live. Jarli, can I borrow your phone?"

Jarli handed it over.

"If you guys or your pilot need a safer hideout," Eaton said as she typed, "call me on this number. I know a place you could use, at least in the short term."

"Thanks."

A ladder was mounted on the tunnel wall. Jarli didn't see it until Eaton pointed. It stretched up and up into the darkness.

"Jarli, this will take you to the industrial district just north of town," she said. "Bess, can you climb ladders?"

Bess looked at the floor.

"I thought not," Eaton said. "You'll have to come with me to the other exit."

"Why can't *I* stay with you?" Jarli asked, trying to keep his voice steady. "Where am I going?"

"The Magnotech factory is a ten-minute walk from the top of this ladder. And the guy who owns the company, Kellin Plowman—"

"Wait. Kellin Plowman owns Magnotech?" Kellin Plowman was the richest person in Kelton, and maybe the state. But Jarli had thought he earned all his money from cryptocurrencies, not magnets.

"He does," Eaton said. "It's an unmanned factory, but I think he often visits. Could be a good place to look for clues about this laser device."

"What about me?" Bess asked.

"I can get you to an exit near Warbydale Farm. No ladders, and it should still be outside the search radius. I can't help any more than that. I should get back to the school before anyone realizes I'm missing and finds my air vent. Rule number three: Keep access points a secret." She met Jarli's gaze. "You won't tell anyone?"

Jarli shook his head.

Eaton looked at Bess.

"You can trust us," Bess said.

Eaton half smiled. "Rule number five. Good luck, Jarli." She gestured up the ladder.

Bess hugged Jarli and then followed Eaton into the darkness, with only a brief glance back. Their footsteps faded away to nothing.

Without them, the dark, enclosed space became unbearable.

Jarli raced up the ladder as though he were being chased by tigers. Once he was a few rungs up, he couldn't see the ground below.

Soon he bumped his head on a metal lid. There was no handle, and it was heavy. Jarli braced his feet against the ladder and pushed with both hands. The lid popped out and grated along the asphalt around the hole.

Jarli poked his head out like a gopher. The manhole was in the middle of a street he didn't immediately recognize. There was no traffic and no parked cars. Just hulking warehouses and abandoned coal refineries behind chain-link fences.

Jarli crawled out of the hole. Now that he was above the surface, his phone pinged. He had missed a call from Mum at two thirty.

He called her back, and she picked up right away. "Jarli! Are you okay?"

It was a relief to hear her voice. "I'm fine," he said. "What about you?"

"We're okay. But you need to come home right away."

"Why?"

"I'll explain when you get here."

"I can't. Some bad people are looking for me. Totally not my fault, by the way."

"That's why you need to come home."

Something in her voice made the hairs on Jarli's arms stand up.

"Mum," he said. "Is someone there with you?"

Silence.

"The people looking for me," Jarli said, "they look like cops. Or maybe they *are* cops, but they're bad. They work for Viper. Are they there? Just answer yes or no."

The line went dead.

Nowhere to Run

As Jarli turned around and around, wondering what to do, he saw two helicopters in the distance. They were circling Kelton's town center like blowflies looking for food.

Other than when a bushfire came too close a few years ago, Jarli had never seen a helicopter in Kelton. These ones were black—not firefighters, not media. More Feds.

Jarli dragged the manhole cover shut. It fell into place with a permanent-sounding *thunk*. He crossed the street and stood in the shade of the only tree on the block. Then he called Dana Reynolds.

She picked up after only two rings. "Jarli. Are you somewhere safe?"

Jarli hesitated. Under a tree in an industrial district didn't seem especially safe. But he wasn't in any immediate danger. "Yes," he said finally.

"Good. I half suspected that you'd sent me on a wild-goose chase," Reynolds said. "But you were right. Journos, criminals, cops—everyone is looking for your friend."

It took Jarli a second to work out that she meant Doug. He still didn't feel like a friend.

"I think the bad guys have my family," Jarli said. "I just called Mum, and it sounded like someone was there."

"Was she at home?"

"Yeah, I think so."

Reynolds sounded excited. "I'm on my way."

Jarli heard a thump as a car door closed. An engine kicked into gear. The sound of Reynolds's voice changed as her phone automatically switched to hands-free.

"I know it doesn't feel like it," she said, "but this is good news. They're exposed. If I can get to your place before they leave, I can get pictures of them. Identify them."

"I don't care about that," Jarli said. "I just want my family to be safe."

"I'll do what I can," Reynolds promised. "Did you know the police have put Kelton on lockdown? They're searching the town and the surrounding lands. They've put checkpoints on the highways. No vehicles can leave town without a thorough inspection. And since you know where Doug is, they're looking for you, too."

"I know," Jarli said. "They were at my school."

"Who was?"

"Two men. They looked like police. Federal. But I think one of them works for Viper."

"That's bad," Reynolds said.

Jarli could see a plume of dust on the horizon. A car was coming. Could be police, or could be no one. Either way, he wanted to get out of sight.

He ran down a narrow alley between two warehouses. Old newspapers blew past like tumbleweeds.

"I've been looking into Steven Fussell," Reynolds was saying. "The passenger who was supposed to board the plane. As far as I can tell, there's no such person. No birth record, no past address, no phone number."

Jarli had to admit that Dana Reynolds was much more than just makeup and big hair. She was good at this spy stuff.

"What does that mean?" Jarli asked.

"Probably just that it's a false name. But I did find a police report. A man named Steven Fussell claimed that he had seen Viper in person and could identify him. The Feds put him on a flight to Kelton."

"Why?"

"That's complicated," Reynolds said. "The magnetic laser is called a reverse coil gun, or RCG. It was manufactured at the Magnotech factory in Kelton, and the cops believe Viper picked it up in person. They wanted to put Fussell in a room with Maayke Cramers—Doug's mother—and show them some security footage. The cops hoped that once Fussell pointed Viper out, Maayke might be able to provide some more details about him. Maybe even his real name. But thanks to his source in the police, Viper got wind of the plan and crashed Fussell's plane into Maayke's house, supposedly killing two birds with one stone."

"But Fussell got wind of *that* plan, so he didn't get on the plane." Jarli's head was starting to hurt. "Why didn't he warn them not to take off?"

"I'm still trying to figure that out," Reynolds said. "I'll keep you posted."

The engine noise got louder and louder. A blue car sped past the alley without slowing down. It was gone too quickly for Jarli to get a good look at it. The engine noise faded away.

"Jarli, you need to stay out of sight for a while," Reynolds said. "Don't trust anyone."

Even you, Jarli thought, remembering Eaton's advice.

A droning sound caught his attention. He looked up, shielding his eyes from the afternoon sun with one hand. One of the helicopters had stopped circling the town and was headed his way.

Jarli felt his insides go watery.

"There's a helicopter coming toward me," he said.

"One of the choppers circling the town?"

"Right. What do I do?"

"They must be tracking your phone. Ditch it and run! Go, now!"

A Rat in a Trap

Even with a helicopter racing toward him, Jarli couldn't bring himself to just throw his phone away. Instead, he quickly buried it under a nearby pile of garbage bags. Maybe he could recover it later. At least whoever was tracking it might waste a few minutes looking for it.

No time to get back to the manhole. Jarli sprinted up the alley, hoping to get out of sight. The whopping of the helicopter blades got louder and louder.

There was a dumpster up ahead, paint flaking off the steel sides. A harsh chemical smell floated around it. The lid was chained shut. Jarli tried to lift it anyway, but he couldn't get it open wide enough to climb through the gap. He kept running.

The warehouse to his left had a roller door. Jarli grabbed the handle at the bottom and pulled. Locked.

He pounded on the shutters. "Hey!" he yelled. "Can anyone hear me? I need help!"

No response from inside. Jarli looked back at the helicopter. It was close enough now that he could see the landing skis and the bulbous windscreen gleaming in the sun. The occupants might not have seen him yet, but they would soon.

He ran out of the alley and turned right, desperate to get out of sight. He found himself on another dusty street. No people, no trees, no open doors. No cover. Locked gates and chain-link fences separated the street from the surrounding buildings.

Most of the fences had barbed wire on top, but one didn't. Behind it was a row of self-storage units and a van with a smashed windscreen. The van was wrapped in police tape like a birthday present.

WHOP-WHOP-WHOP. The helicopter was getting closer. Jarli ran over and started climbing the fence. The wire rattled, digging into his hands and leaving red creases on his fingers as he scrambled over the top. He dropped down on the other side and crawled under the smashed-up van.

There wasn't as much room as he had expected. Even with his face pressed against the concrete, the undercarriage of the van—black metal spattered with oil and dirt—was only centimeters above his head.

Jarli lay still, his heart pounding. He didn't know what to do next. He was trapped. If he ran in any direction, he would be visible from the air. He was still in his cheery blue school uniform. And he had no phone now, so he couldn't call any-one for help.

The engine noise from the helicopter rose to a deafening shriek—

Then four ropes appeared, dangling over the street. There was a zipping sound as four people slid down the ropes and landed on the asphalt.

Each of them wore black combat fatigues and tough-looking boots. Their faces were invisible behind helmets with mirrored visors.

All four were carrying machine guns. Jarli was terrified. He'd never seen a machine gun in real life. Were these people Federal Police, or were they working for Viper? Or both?

The four ropes slithered up out of sight. The helicopter noise faded as the aircraft moved away. Nobody spoke. One of the police—actually, they looked more like soldiers—went left up the street. Another went right. The other two disappeared into the alley.

Jarli trembled. If they were tracking his phone, they would find it soon. They would realize that he had ditched it and that he was hiding nearby. Jarli had to get out of here.

He scrambled out from under the van and ran toward the row of self-storage units. They looked like garages and probably contained the same stuff—tax files, old computers, cobwebs, and dust. Surely someone would have left one unlocked.

Jarli reached the first unit. The roller door was padlocked closed. So was the next. And the next.

The fourth unit along was locked just like the others. But

the padlock had a three-digit combination rather than a keyhole. Jarli used a padlock just like this on his locker at school. Whenever he closed it, he rotated one of the number wheels a single notch, so it was easy to open again. Maybe the owner of this unit was equally lazy.

Jarli crouched down and squinted at the padlock. The wheels were set at 7-2-4. He turned one, so the combination read 6-2-4. The padlock wouldn't open. He tried 8-2-4. No luck. 7-1-4. Nothing. 7-3-4. Still nothing.

Then a different door rolled open in the opposite row.

Jarli whirled around, expecting to see a stranger cleaning out a locker—or one of Viper's soldiers, who had somehow gotten behind him.

He saw neither of those things.

The person staring at him from inside the storage unit was Doug.

Bunker Down

arli?" Doug said. He was wearing a big coat and carrying a heavy bag. "What are you doing here?"

"We have to hide," Jarli said. "People are after me!"

Doug looked around, confused. Jarli pushed past him into the storage unit.

"Close the door," he said. "Quick!"

Doug hurriedly pulled the roller door shut, plunging the unit into darkness.

"Who's after you?" Doug asked. "The hazmat suit guys?"

"I don't know," Jarli said. "There's four of them now. They have a helicopter and guns. The whole shebang. They might be police—Dana Reynolds says they have Kelton locked down."

"I know," Doug said. "Guys in police uniforms were searching near the cave. I can't go back there."

"Where's Priya?"

"When I woke up, she was gone. I assumed she'd ignored your journalist friend's advice and gone looking for the cops. Reynolds didn't mention her?"

"No," Jarli said. "But if she'd found the police, I think Reynolds would have heard about it."

"So Viper must have caught her," Doug said grimly.

"What is this place?" Jarli asked.

"My parents' storage unit." Doug flicked a switch. Neon bulbs stuttered to life, illuminating the inside of the unit. It was mostly empty. Plastic crates were lined up on skeletal metal shelves. A skin of dust covered everything.

"I was hoping Mum and Dad might be here," Doug said. "Maybe they'd forgotten about meeting me at the underpass, or maybe they were there while I was looking for Priya with you."

"Any sign that they've been here?" Jarli asked.

"No." Doug looked tired, and moved like he was sore. Life on the run was hard—Jarli wondered how much longer they could last.

The plastic crates had transparent sides. Inside Jarli saw clothes, bandages, radios, and new phones still in their boxes.

"Did Reynolds give you anything useful?" Doug asked.

"She said Viper had collected the laser device from the Magnotech factory near Kelton. She thought there might be footage of him on the surveillance cameras." He was about to tell Doug that Nurse Eaton had also mentioned the factory, but he had promised not to tell anyone about the secret tunnel out of her office. So he said nothing.

"Let's eat something and then check it out," Doug said. He

pulled two granola bars and a burner phone out of the box and started setting it up. "I'll get the address."

"We can't go now," Jarli said. "Those guys are looking for us."

"You just said Viper was listening in on your phone call, right?"

"I think so. The helicopter started chasing me pretty much as soon as I started talking."

"So Viper knows that we know about the factory," he said.

Jarli saw what Doug was getting at. "You think he'll try to get there first? Destroy the evidence?"

"Yes. If we don't break into the factory soon, there'll be nothing to find."

"Break into the factory?" Jarli could barely believe what he was hearing. "We're kids. The police are looking for us. And *I* don't know how to steal video from a security camera. Do you?"

Doug was peering down at the phone. "I have the address," he announced. He opened one of the plastic crates. Inside were tan stockings, rolls of duct tape, gloves, a pair of bolt cutters, and something that looked like a garage door remote. His parents clearly had a broad definition of "emergency supplies."

Doug pulled one of the stockings over his face. It smoothed his features, making him look like a shop-window mannequin.

"You really think we can do this?" Jarli asked.

Doug's serious eyes stared at Jarli through the fabric. "I really think we don't have a choice."

The sun was getting low, stretching shadows across the streets of the industrial district. The air temperature had plummeted. A washed-out moon was already visible in the pink sky.

They were in a hurry, but they had to move carefully. The helicopter was still around. Jarli could hear it searching the streets on the other side of a nearby warehouse.

Doug unlocked the main gate of the storage facility and slipped out into the street. Jarli followed him up past the alley with the dumpster. He wondered if his phone was still there, or if the bad guys had found it already. They ran uphill past a tire shop, a takeaway restaurant, and a funeral home. All looked abandoned. None of the billboards on the street had current advertisers; they all said things like YOUR AD COULD BE HERE! and GET YOUR BUSINESS NOTICED!

At the top of the hill stood a steel bench that might once have been a bus stop. Transparent plastic barriers on either side protected it from the wind, with bolts at the top for a missing roof. As they ran past it, Doug hissed, "Get down!" and pulled Jarli off his feet.

Jarli hit the concrete and scrabbled under the bench. "What is it?"

"Look." Doug pointed down the other side of the hill. At the bottom was a large, white building with round walls and a flat top. Chimneys dotted the roof like candles on a birthday cake. A sign on one wall said MAGNOTECH.

But that wasn't what Doug was pointing at. He had spotted two of the soldiers from the helicopter walking up the slope toward them, away from the building. Their steps were quiet and stealthy. One of them had holstered his machine gun, but the other kept hers raised. Both were slowly turning their heads from side to side, like clown statues in a carnival game.

Looking for us, Jarli thought.

"We have to go back," he whispered. But when he turned, he saw the helicopter hovering above the storage facility. If they went back, they'd be spotted.

Jarli looked around, increasingly frantic. A wall to the right, an alley to the left—but the alley was a dead end. They were trapped.

"Hide in the alley until they go past," Jarli whispered.

"They'll see us."

"There's no other way."

Doug was digging through his bag. He pulled out a black plastic square with a single rubber button—the object Jarli had thought was a garage door remote. The words on the side read, PERSONAL SAFETY ALARM.

"Block your ears," Doug whispered. Then he pushed the button, hurled the device down the alleyway, and crouched back down under the bench.

Jarli barely had time to clap his palms over his ears before a piercing shriek filled the air. It sounded like a smoke alarm. Even through his hands, the volume made it hard to think.

The shrieking alarm faded and the pitch seemed to descend as the device soared through the air, bounced on the concrete, and skittered out of sight down the alley.

It was a much more high-tech distraction than Jarli's rock.

The soldiers reacted fast, clomping up the hill toward the entrance to the alleyway. They probably thought the noise was a car alarm. But it wouldn't take them long to realize that there were no cars, and the alley was a dead end.

As soon as the soldiers entered the alley, Doug nudged Jarli. They both crawled out from behind the bench and raced down the hill toward the factory.

The driveway was blocked by a heavy steel gate. The rest of the building was surrounded by a chain-link fence protected by thick bollards. It was designed to withstand attacks by large vehicles, but not teenagers with bolt cutters. Doug snipped through the links, and he and Jarli slipped through the gap.

Breaking and entering. Jarli could almost hear Constable Blanco saying the words. It was one thing to muck around with computer viruses or duck under police tape, but slicing through a fence to access private property felt much more criminal.

Before, Jarli had only worried about what would happen

if they failed. Now he wondered what would happen if they succeeded. Even if they identified Viper without getting caught by his secret army, wouldn't they still get in trouble with the police?

Doug didn't seem worried. "Come on," he whispered.

Beyond the fence was a solar array—a huge network of shiny panels bolted to a grid of metal pipes. Jarli and Doug made their way through, stepping over cables. Jarli felt like an ant crawling across a microchip. The panels were so densely clustered that the fence was soon out of sight. At least the soldiers wouldn't see them from the top of the hill.

"Nice to see that this evil megacorporation uses renewable energy," Jarli said as they wove through the network of panels.

"Magnotech isn't evil," Doug said.

"Didn't they make the laser that shot down the plane?"

"Yeah, but they didn't know how it was going to be used. Viper is the real bad guy."

Jarli wondered if Doug was being defensive because his mother had worked for Magnotech. Any company that made weapons without asking questions sounded pretty evil to Jarli.

"Those aren't solar panels, though," Doug added. "They're mirrors."

"Mirrors?" Jarli peered around the side of one. A curved version of his own face stared back.

"Yeah. When we first moved here, I looked up the satellite feed over Kelton. There was a bright white spot over the industrial district. Now I know what it was. These mirrors reflect the sunlight back up into the sky, too bright for passing satellites to see through."

Jarli didn't have time to ask why a non-evil company would be worried about satellite surveillance. The conversation was interrupted by a humming sound like a small lawn mower.

"A drone," Doug whispered. "Hide!"

They ducked under the nearest mirror. As the humming got louder and louder, the mirror started to swivel. Jarli had to crab-walk to stay under it. All the other mirrors turned in unison.

The humming stayed loud and close. It sounded like the drone was hovering right above them.

Jarli held his breath, wondering what would happen if it spotted them. Would it shoot? Did it have weapons? He couldn't risk peeking. Maybe it was just a flying camera, one that could summon the soldiers.

The sound faded. The drone was moving away. The mirrors shifted back into place.

"Midflight recharge," Doug said. "Clever."

Jarli's heart was still racing. "What?"

"When the mirrors realigned, I'm pretty sure they were all pointed at the drone. It must use concentrated bursts of sunlight to recharge the batteries so it can keep flying around this building forever without landing. I've heard of laser recharging, but never solar. Pretty cool, really."

"So it wasn't looking for us?" Jarli asked. "You think it's just guarding this facility?"

"Right," Doug said. "Like a surveillance camera that can move around."

Jarli was feeling worse and worse about sneaking into this facility, which was invisible from the air and protected by flying robots. But it was too late to turn back.

"We should keep moving," he said.

"Okay, but keep an ear out. I doubt they only built one drone."

Uneasily, Jarli followed Doug toward the building.

"So you know about this stuff?" he said. "Machines and technology?"

"Yeah. I used to do competitions back home. Robot fights, you know? Two robots try to smash each other. I was building a really cool robot, but I had to leave it behind when I moved. You ever do anything like that?"

Jarli shook his head. "No. I'm no good at hardware—only software. I can write the code to make a computer do just about anything, but I can't build the computer itself."

"I'm the opposite," Doug said. "It's a pity we didn't know each other back home. We could have made a good team. Rebecca's robot would have been toast."

"Who's Rebecca?" Jarli asked. But Doug didn't respond, and soon they had reached the edge of the solar array.

The building had two doors. One was polished glass in a

steel frame, facing a parking lot. Jarli guessed this was the door customers entered through, but it was after five o'clock, so the doors were locked. The lights inside were off, making the glass like a mirror.

The other door turned out to be hidden around the curved side of the building. It was a square of painted metal on hydraulic hinges, big enough to drive a truck through. There didn't seem to be a way to open the big square door. No keyhole, no keypad, no handle. Maybe it could only be opened from inside.

While they were scoping out the place, Jarli noticed something. The helicopter noise had stopped. He peeked between the solar panels. No sign of the aircraft. Maybe it had landed. Perhaps it was refueling. Maybe the soldiers had given up. They went back around to the front, where the glass door was.

"We'll have to smash the glass," Doug was saying.

"Won't the alarms go off?"

"Yeah, but all the lights are out. And didn't you say it was an unmanned factory? I reckon no one's here. They wouldn't have drones *and* security guards, would they?"

"The alarm will summon somebody," Jarli said. "Like an off-site security team. When they see the smashed door, they'll search the building."

"Then we'll have to grab what we need and get out before they arrive."

That sounded like a bad plan to Jarli. He wasn't even sure they'd be able to find the computer with the video files on it, let alone get the files off it somehow. They needed more time.

"I have a better idea," he said. "See that blinking light?"

Doug looked. They couldn't see much through the glass doors, but there was a single red light somewhere up high.

"I bet that's a smoke alarm," Jarli said. "And I bet if it goes off, the doors will unlock. That's the law, right?"

"Yeah, but someone will turn up. Like you said."

"It will be the fire department, though. Not a security team. They'll look around, make sure there's no fire, and then leave. After that, we'll have as much time as we need."

"The door looks airtight," Doug said. "How can we set off the smoke alarm if we can't get to it?"

"With these." Jarli grabbed one of the big mirrors and swiveled it. The hinges creaked, and a shaft of fading sunlight fell across the door. "A concentrated burst of sunlight, right at the smoke alarm. Or at the carpet underneath it, or something."

A smile spread across Doug's face. "Ooh, that's clever. I like that."

"Help me with the mirrors," Jarli said. "We don't have much daylight left."

They worked as quickly as they could, swiveling mirrors to face the doorway. The foyer with the smoke alarm became brighter as more and more sunlight was focused on it. Soon they couldn't see it at all—the glass door was too bright to look at.

Doug turned the last available mirror. "Do you think it's working?" he asked.

"I don't know." Jarli walked toward the glass door and then hurriedly jumped back as the beam of sunlight scorched his skin. It was like suddenly opening a hot oven. He couldn't get close enough to see into the foyer.

"We just have to wait, I guess," he said, still smarting from the sunburn.

And then the steel gates started to squeak open in the distance. Someone was here.

Into the Dark

Jarli and Doug froze. They couldn't see the gates through the forest of mirrors, but they could hear tires coming up the driveway.

"The security team is here," Jarli hissed. "The drone must have spotted us."

"Get back to the fence," Doug said. "Quick!"

As they ran back the way they had come, the humming sound returned. They both froze under the cover of one of the mirrors. The drone was right overhead.

"We're trapped," Jarli whispered.

The car—or van, or whatever it was—stopped in the parking lot. Someone jumped out. Two people, it sounded like.

"Forget the drone," Doug said quietly. "If it sees us, it sees us. We have to get out of here, now."

"Wait," Jarli said.

"But we—"

"Just wait." Jarli could hear the two men running, but not toward the solar array.

They were headed for the building.

"If the drone saw us," Jarli said, "why are they going toward the building?"

"Maybe they think we're inside."

"Or maybe they're not the security team."

The drone noise faded away to nothing. Jarli leaned over, peeking out from behind the mirror panel. Two people were fiddling with the glass door. They didn't seem to have noticed the concentrated sunlight—

Because they were both wearing hazmat suits.

"Viper's men are here," Jarli hissed. "To destroy the evidence, like you said. They'll be removing the footage of him from the cameras."

Doug's eyes widened. "Oh, no. We're too late!"

"Maybe not."

"What do you mean?"

The two men had unlocked the door somehow. One of them must have had a code or a key card. The glass slid open with a hiss, and they slipped through into the darkness.

Jarli crept out from under the mirror. He could see the black van in the parking lot, the same one from the crash site. The driver's seat was empty. And the drone still hadn't come back. No one would notice him.

"Jarli!" Doug whispered. "What are you doing?"

The glass door was already starting to close.

Jarli ran across the parking lot toward it. No time to be careful or quiet. His feet pounded the concrete. His own breaths were deafening in his ears.

The door was almost completely shut. When Jarli was two or three meters from it, he hit the blazing beam of sunlight and bit back a scream. Dropping to the ground, he threw himself under the light and slid feetfirst toward the doorway, the concrete scraping his back through his clothes.

He managed to get one foot inside the building just before the door fully closed. The door pressed his shoe against the frame, hard. For a split second, Jarli thought it was going to cut half his foot off. Then the door sensed the blockage and retreated.

Jarli peered through into the dark. No sign of the two men in hazmat suits. But he didn't want to risk calling out to Doug. He just beckoned instead.

Doug was already swiveling mirrors back the other way, dispersing the sunlight. When he was done, he ran over.

"You're crazy!" he whispered. But he was grinning.

"I'm crazy?" Jarli demanded. "*You're* crazy! This whole thing was your idea."

"Well, yeah. But anyway, I'm glad that you're with me."

It was the nicest thing Jarli had ever heard Doug say. "Thanks, Doug."

"My real name's Terence."

Jarli was surprised. "You don't look like a Terence."

Doug—Terence—looked uncomfortable. "Come on. We've got to get that surveillance footage before Viper's guys destroy it."

They slipped into the building.

PART THREE
THE LEIDENFROST
EFFECT

For a long time, the polygraph machine was the gold standard in lie detection. It measured skin conductivity, blood pressure, and other things. It was good at determining if the subject was nervous—but liars aren't always nervous, and nervous people aren't always lying.

—*Documentation from* Truth, *version 2.3*

Deadly Lake

As his eyes adjusted, Jarli saw a curved reception desk, a leather couch, and a framed poster: MAGNOTECH. WE'RE MAGNANIMOUS! In the picture, a train appeared to be floating above the rails.

The glass door slid closed behind them. Instinctively, Jarli looked for a way to open it again. But there was no handle and no button. Just a keyhole. They were stuck in here, unless they set off the smoke alarm.

And when Jarli looked up, he saw that the blinking light in the ceiling wasn't a smoke alarm after all. It was a camera sealed in a dark glass bubble. Jarli could feel it watching him.

"Can you get the footage of Viper from that?" Doug asked. Jarli still struggled to think of him as "Terence."

"No," Jarli said. "It wouldn't have its own hard drive. It'll send the files to a computer somewhere. And the computer may not even be in this building."

"Viper clearly thinks it is," Doug pointed out. "He sent his guys here. Makes sense—Magnotech is super paranoid about leaks. Mum wasn't even allowed to take her phone to work. This factory might not have an Internet connection."

Jarli nodded slowly. This was called "air-gapping"—keeping a system secure by severing all connections to the outside world. His dad's old employer, CipherCrypt, had used an air-gapped system to stop hackers getting in and prevent dangerous viruses from escaping onto the Internet. And CipherCrypt had worked for Viper, just like Magnotech.

On the other side of the reception desk, a plastic potted plant had been dragged across the carpet to prop open a door. Probably the work of the hazmat guys.

Doug and Jarli climbed over the desk and crept through the door into a corridor. With every step, Jarli got colder and colder. He found himself rubbing his arms and shivering.

"You feel that?" Doug asked. It sounded like his teeth were chattering.

"Yeah. Why is it so cold in here?"

"Some metals are more magnetic at low temperatures. Maybe this place needs to be cold while they make them."

At the end of the corridor was an open doorway leading to a steel catwalk. It was suspended from the ceiling about two meters above the factory floor. Jarli could see rows upon rows of machines—giant metal arms poised over conveyor belts. Lamps swayed on long chains like flying saucers. Only one of them was switched on.

Jarli didn't freak out until he looked down.

The factory floor was hidden beneath a veil of mist that rolled and rippled like a white ocean.

"What is that?" he whispered.

Doug was peering over the edge of the catwalk, fascinated. "Liquid nitrogen," he said. "Whatever's down there, they must need to keep it *really* cold. Don't fall in. You'd turn into a block of ice in seconds."

"No kidding." Jarli already felt like a block of ice. His hands and feet were numb. "Is it safe to breathe?"

"Yeah. Nitrogen isn't toxic. It makes up most of the air on Earth, I think."

Even so, Jarli didn't like the look of the mist rising off the white pool. Then he spotted something on one of the conveyor belts just above the nitrogen pool. It was a box with a tube protruding out one side, about the size of a data projector. Just like the object he had seen in the wreckage of Doug's house.

"Doug," Jarli said. "You ever seen something like that before?"

Doug peered down at the conveyor belt. "No. Why?"

"I think it's the device. The one Viper used to bring down the plane. Reynolds called it an RCG—a reverse coil gun."

"Why do you think that's what it is?"

Jarli was figuring it out as he spoke. "If it works like a big magnet, pulling the plane down, it would have needed to be at the house, right? Viper probably hid it in your backyard.

But he wouldn't have wanted anyone to find it afterward and realize what he had done. I think he sent those two guys to collect it. I saw them pick up something exactly like that from the wreckage."

"So why is it here? Getting repaired?"

"No, I reckon that's a new one. The one at the house was pretty smashed." As the mist cleared, Jarli saw a second device on the conveyor belt. Then a third. A fourth.

Doug had seen them too. "Why would Magnotech be making new ones?"

"Maybe Viper ordered more, now that he knows the prototype works. It's an unmanned factory—the robots probably started building the devices automatically as soon as Viper placed the order."

"Why haven't the police stopped production? Wouldn't they be watching the factory?"

"Maybe they are," Jarli said. "Maybe they think they can catch Viper when he picks the RCGs up."

"But some police secretly work for Viper," Doug said. "So he probably has a plan to avoid getting caught. This is bad." He ran a hand through his hair. "This is so bad."

He was right. There were enough RCGs here to crash a dozen planes. Maybe more, if they could be used more than once. And Jarli doubted that the next plane to crash would be empty.

He shivered. "Let's find what we need and get out of here."

The far end of the catwalk split off in two directions. The right-hand side led downstairs. Jarli thought it probably went to a loading dock—it was the same side of the building as the big square door he'd seen earlier.

The other side of the intersection went upstairs to a door marked CONTROL ROOM—UNAUTHORIZED ACCESS PROHIBITED.

"You reckon that might be where the computers are?" Doug asked.

"Worth a shot," Jarli said. "But keep an eye out for Viper's people."

They hurried up the catwalk, the metal grille clanking under their feet. When they reached the control room door, Jarli pressed his ear to it.

He couldn't hear anything inside. But that didn't mean the hazmat-suit guys weren't in there. Surely the control room was the first place they would look.

There was a window, but Jarli couldn't peer through it without leaning over the edge of the catwalk, above the deadly ocean of liquid nitrogen. Instead, he twisted the door handle, slowly. It moved without a squeak.

He opened the door just a crack. Warm air flooded through the gap. Darkness inside. If the hazmat guys were in there, they hadn't turned on the lights.

Jarli listened for a moment longer, then he eased his body through the gap. The room came into focus. There were two desks, a filing cabinet, and an air vent in the ceiling—too narrow for a person to hide in. No sign of the hazmat guys.

But there was a desktop computer.

Jarli beckoned to Doug, who slipped in and closed the door behind him. Jarli switched on the computer. As it booted up, he checked the back. Only four cords were plugged in: power, monitor, keyboard, mouse. No LAN cable, so it was probably air-gapped. Which hopefully meant not much security. No need to install anti-hacking software on a computer that wasn't connected to the Internet, right?

The screen lit up, and a login prompt appeared.

Username:

KPlowman

Password:

"How long will this take?" Doug asked.

"Try to find a password," Jarli said. "People often write it down somewhere near the machine."

"That's dumb."

"Yes, but people do it."

While Doug was searching the room, Jarli tried a few common passwords. *Password. ABCDEFGH. 12345678. 87654321.*

"There's nothing written down," Doug said, still looking through the filing cabinet. "But I found these keys."

Jarli took the key ring. It had four wide keys on it. Nothing was engraved on them, but it seemed likely that one of them would open the front door.

Jarli clicked the forgotten password link. Two security questions popped up.

Your birthday:

Your mother's maiden name:

"Did you bring that new phone with you?" he asked.

"Yeah." Doug unlocked it and passed it over. "Why?"

Jarli was already bringing up a social networking app. "I'm hoping Kellin Plowman isn't careful with what he posts online."

Plowman *was* careful. But his family wasn't. When Jarli found Kellin's profile—unlisted but not private—he found a post from Adrian Plowman, on October 20. *Happy birthday, little brother!*

In a list of Kellin and Adrian's mutual friends, Jarli found their mother, Sheryl Plowman. A lot of her friends had the surname Goldacre.

Jarli checked Plowman's age on a business news site. Then he typed:

Your birthday:
OCTOBER 20, 1978

Your mother's maiden name:

GOLDACRE

The computer was air-gapped, so it couldn't text the new password to Plowman's phone. Instead, the new password just appeared on the screen.

Doug was watching over Jarli's shoulder. "Wow," he said. "It wouldn't be that easy to get into *my* computer, would it?"

"Easier, probably." Jarli was searching the computer's files. But there were thousands of videos, each hours long. And Viper's guys could come in at any moment.

"Do you know what date Viper came here to pick up the device?" Jarli asked.

Doug shook his head. "I know it was meant to be ready in March last year."

Jarli found the videos from March. But the facility had at least four cameras, and each one was recording twenty-four hours per day. There was way too much data to sift through.

"I have a flash drive," Doug said. "We can sort through it all later."

Jarli had a flash drive too—the one he kept on his key chain and had used in last night's coding experiments. But it only had sixty-four gigabytes of space. "There are too many videos, and they're too big," he said. "We'd need a hundred flash drives—"

Then the alarms went off.

Drone Warfare

Doug and Jarli looked at each other. Doug looked as scared as Jarli felt.

"They know we're here," Jarli hissed.

"Or they know Viper's guys are here," Doug said. "Either way, we need to get gone. Can we just take the whole computer with us?"

Jarli tried to lift it. It didn't budge. It was bolted in place. "Do you have a screwdriver? Maybe we can rip out the hard drive." Jarli didn't know how to do that, but he thought Doug might.

Doug was about to reply when a buzzing sound filled the air. Jarli looked out the window in time to see four drones enter the factory through a vent in the ceiling. Each one had four rotors and a bubble camera on the underside. With unnerving precision, they turned in midair and flew in different directions. Two flew over the nitrogen lake, scanning it with red lasers. Another flew down to the loading dock.

The last one flew up toward the control room.

"That's not good," Doug said.

He and Jarli both ducked down under the desk as the drone approached the window. A scanning laser swept across the room.

"Can they get in here?" Jarli whispered.

"I don't think so. But we can't just wait for them to go away. A human security team will arrive soon."

He was right. There was no time to disassemble the computer and take the hard drive. They had to get out of here.

Timing his movements to avoid the scanning laser, Jarli leaned out from under the desk and jammed his flash drive into the computer. He couldn't take all the video files from last March, but he could take a few. Maybe he would get lucky and Viper would be in one of them.

The monitor flashed.

UNVERIFIED PUBLISHER

Do you want to install the following program on this computer?

Program name: picsaver.exe
Publisher: unknown
File origin: Removable disk E:

YES/NO

OUROBOROS, the virus Jarli had used to test his firewall,

was still on the flash drive. The virus designed to copy every file on a computer.

The idea hit Jarli so hard it nearly knocked him over. He clicked YES.

The drone at the window moved away. Jarli motioned for Doug to come out from under the table.

"When you took this phone out of the box," he asked Doug, "did you grab the charger cable?"

"Yeah." Doug pulled it out of his pocket and handed it over. Jarli used it to plug the phone into one of the USB ports at the back of the computer.

"What are you doing?" Doug asked.

Jarli was tethering the phone to the computer. *Hey, presto, no more air gap.* Once the computer was connected to the Internet, the virus would copy the whole hard drive to the server in India. With a bit of luck, Jarli could hack that server later, and steal the files back. Probably. Maybe. Hopefully. But all that was too difficult to explain right now. "The phone is e-mailing the files to me," he said, simplifying things a bit. "It'll take hours, though. We'll have to leave it here. What's the data cap?"

A green check mark flashed up on the screen.

>>*Your computer is now connected.*

"There's no data cap," Doug said. "Mum wanted to make sure it would always work in an emergency."

"Well, this is an emergency." Jarli tucked the phone out of sight behind the computer. There was no way to tell if his plan was working, since the virus was invisible. He hoped it would transmit all the files before Plowman found it.

"Okay." Jarli pulled out the flash drive and pocketed it. "I'm done. How do we get out of here?"

"We can't go back out the front. The drones will spot us. We'll have to go downstairs to the garage exit."

"Any sign of the hazmat-suit guys?"

Doug peered out the window. "No."

This was supposed to be good news, but it felt like bad news. If Viper's people weren't here, they were probably in the loading dock. And if they had come here to delete the videos on the computer, why hadn't they gone to the control room?

Jarli wondered if he and Doug were too late. Maybe the bad guys had gone up to the control room, logged into the computer, deleted the file with Viper in it, shut the computer down again, and escaped through the garage, all while Jarli and Doug were making their way in through reception. Had there been enough time for that? Jarli didn't think so. But then where were they?

Jarli went to go out the door, but Doug grabbed him.

"Wait," he said. He was watching the drones circle out the window. If they moved at the wrong moment, they could still be spotted.

"Wait," Doug said again. "Wait . . . now!"

Jarli wrenched open the door and they both rushed out. The cold was so sudden that it was like stepping into the vacuum of space. Even knowing that the drones couldn't hear him, Jarli cringed as his footsteps clattered on the metal stairs.

One of the drones was zooming over the nitrogen lake toward them. The camera bubble was beneath it rather than on the front. Jarli wondered how close it would have to get before they were spotted.

They sprinted across the T-intersection and dashed down the staircase toward the garage. The drone whined as it got closer and closer.

The farther down they went, the colder it was. The stairs descended below the factory floor, and a pane of glass separated the bottom half of the staircase from the liquid nitrogen. Fine mist trickled over the pane and poured down the stairs. Through the glass, Jarli could see that the nitrogen lake was only about thirty centimeters deep. It was strange how much it looked like normal water. Under the mist, the floor was lined with pipes, frosted at the joins.

The door at the bottom of the stairs was marked LOADING DOCK. It wasn't locked. Jarli and Doug pushed through. Jarli shut the door behind them. He tried to do it quietly—Viper's people might be here—but the sound echoed around the concrete room.

The loading dock was a cavernous space filled with large wooden crates. A crowbar lay in the middle of the floor near a smaller crate, as though someone had abandoned it in a hurry. Cardboard boxes were tightly packed on metal shelves. The big square door Jarli had seen looked no less daunting from the inside.

Doug ran over to it. "How do you think we get this open?" he asked. "I don't see a button."

Jarli dug the keys from the control room out of his pocket, but he couldn't find a keyhole anywhere. "Maybe with the crowbar," he said. The crowbar was heavy, but he could lift it. Hopefully it was strong enough to do the job.

Something beeped inside the small crate.

Jarli hesitated.

"Come on," Doug said. "Bring it here."

Jarli ignored him. One wall of the crate wasn't attached—it was just leaning against the sides. He grabbed it and pulled.

"What are you doing?" Doug demanded.

The wall of the crate clattered to the ground, revealing the interior.

There was another beep, and this time Jarli saw what had made it.

A timer. Attached by thin wires to a lump of what looked like yellow clay.

The timer read, 01:19. Now 01:18.

01:17.

01:16.

Countdown to Danger

W hat's that?" Doug's face was ashen.

"A bomb!" Jarli's mind was racing. Viper's people hadn't come to delete the files. They were going to blow up the whole building. Every computer, every camera, every trace of the magnetic devices.

The timer had reached 01:08.

"What do we do?" Doug cried.

"Get the garage door open!"

"I can't!"

Doug was right. Jarli still had the keys in his hand, but he couldn't see a keyhole or a button anywhere. He jammed the crowbar under the door and pulled. It wouldn't budge. Doug grabbed the crowbar as well, but even with their combined strength, they couldn't move the door.

"We'll have to go out the front way," Doug puffed.

"There's no time!" They would have to run up the stairs, across the catwalk, through reception, and figure out how to open the front door, all in the space of a minute. Even that might not get them outside the blast radius. The bad guys clearly expected the blast to destroy the control room, which was all the way upstairs. The bomb must have a lot of explosive power. And it would go off in *fifty-eight seconds*.

"Do you know how to defuse a bomb?" Jarli asked hopefully.

"Why would I know that?!"

"I don't know! I thought maybe you might have made a bomb disposal robot or something."

Jarli had played a video game that involved bomb disposal. But the bomb in the game hadn't looked anything like this. And there had been no wire cutting anyway. The player had used a special spray to freeze the bomb.

"Freeze the bomb . . ." An idea formed in Jarli's head. He peered at the explosive, trying to see if it was attached to anything. It didn't look like it was. The timer was at 00:47 now.

He carefully lifted the bomb. It was strange to think that something so light could have so much destructive power.

"What are you doing?" Doug demanded.

"We have to freeze it!" Jarli hurried back toward the stairs, carrying the bomb as carefully as a carton of eggs. The lump of plastic explosive was pressed against his chest. If the bomb went off, he'd be vaporized.

The timer was at 00:31.

"Open the door for me," Jarli said. "Quick!"

Doug did. "This isn't going to work."

"It's our only shot." Jarli ran halfway up the stairs and

leaned over the glass. The liquid nitrogen bubbled less than half a meter below. It was so cold.

He hesitated. What if dropping the bomb into the lake set it off somehow?

The timer was at 00:12. He was out of options.

Doug was shaking. "This isn't going to work!" he yelled again.

Ignoring him, Jarli dropped the bomb into the liquid nitrogen.

It landed with a splash and sank like a brick. Jarli watched through the glass as the bomb hit the bottom. For a second it seemed to be shrink-wrapped in a thin layer of air, but then the air bubbled away to nothing.

The screen of the timer cracked, and the countdown disappeared. Frost spread across the wires. The yellow clay turned white at the corners.

Jarli held his breath.

Nothing happened.

"Did it work?" Doug asked finally.

Jarli exhaled. "I think so. Wow, that was scary."

"I can't believe it. We should get out of here, just in case it goes off anyway." Doug peered through the glass. "Hey, are those the keys?"

"What?" Jarli looked. His jaw fell open. Yes, there they were—the keys from the control room, lying next to the bomb. He'd still had them in his hand when he picked up the bomb. He must have dropped them into the liquid nitrogen when he threw the bomb in. Now they were inaccessible.

"Oh. Whoops," he said.

"Whoops?! How are we supposed to get out of here?"

"Uh . . ." Jarli looked around. "Maybe we could use the crowbar."

Doug ran back down to the loading dock and then returned carrying the crowbar. "Geez, this thing's heavy."

He dipped the crowbar into the liquid nitrogen. Jarli watched, teeth chattering, as the curved point scraped across the floor toward the keys. The mist washed over them.

"Don't breathe," Doug said.

"You said nitrogen wasn't toxic!"

"Yeah, but it displaces oxygen. If you completely fill your lungs up with it, you'll pass out."

It was no good. The end of the crowbar was too wide to fit through the key ring. Doug could drag the keys over to the glass-like barrier, but he couldn't lift them.

"Let me try," Jarli said.

A red light flashed.

Jarli immediately looked at the bomb, but that wasn't where the flash had come from. Something was whining above him. Jarli had been so distracted by the bomb that he hadn't noticed it until now.

"Drone!" Doug yelled.

The drone descended like a pterosaur. The whining turbines blasted Jarli with cold air.

"Get down!" Doug yelled, and he swung the crowbar like a baseball bat. The bar clipped one side of the drone, sending it spinning away across the ice-cold factory floor.

"They know we're here," Doug said. "We need those keys!"

"I have an idea," Jarli said.

"Whatever it is, do it quick," Doug said.

"I think I can just reach in and grab the keys."

Doug stared at him. "It's liquid nitrogen, Jarli. It's minus two hundred degrees. It'll freeze your hand off."

"Not if I'm quick," Jarli said. "Did you see the bubble of air around the bomb as it sank? We talked about this in chemistry class. My skin will heat up the nitrogen, making a protective glove of gas. For a second or two, at least. It's called the . . . something-or-other effect."

"I think your brain is frozen," Doug said. "There's no way the gas will protect you long enough for you to grab those keys."

"We have to try." Jarli's trembling hand was poised over the liquid nitrogen. He told himself this would work.

"One," he said, "two . . . three!"

Magnetic Warp

J ust as Jarli was about to dip his hand into the nitrogen,
Doug pulled him away from the edge.

"Wait," Doug said. "I have a better idea."

"Thank God." Jarli let the air out of his lungs. His heart
was racing. "What is it?"

Doug ran back up to the catwalk and leaned over the edge.
The crowbar was just long enough to reach one of the conveyor belts below. He hooked the end through the cabling on
one of the RCG devices, and tried to lift it.

"It's too heavy," he grunted.

Jarli ran up and grabbed the crowbar. Together they
hauled the RCG up onto the catwalk. The box was made
of thick plastic, ice-cold. It burned Jarli's hands when he
touched it. He was suddenly glad he hadn't dipped his hand
into the nitrogen.

"Now what?" he asked, panting.

"Now we work out how to switch it on." Doug was already
looking at the controls. There were about twenty buttons on
the side, some already glowing. The device may not have

been finished, but at least it had a pre-charged battery.

"Huh," Doug said, fascinated. "It's not one magnet, it's a whole sequence of them. They switch on and off so fast that they create a focused magnetic field, which pulls—"

"You want to use a magnet powerful enough to take down an airplane," Jarli said, "to fetch a set of keys?"

"Safer than sticking your hand in liquid nitrogen." Doug carried the RCG back along the catwalk until he was directly above the keys. He pushed a button, and the machine started to hum—a sound so deep it made the air throb. Ripples quivered across the nitrogen lake. The laser made a blue dot below.

"Do you know what you're doing?" Jarli asked as Doug aimed the machine at the keys.

"Nope." Doug pushed another button.

The hum got louder. The catwalk shook under Jarli's feet.

"Uh, Doug?" he said. "I mean, Terence? Maybe you should turn it off."

"Just a minute," Doug said.

The keys burst out of the nitrogen and hurtled upward, leaving a trail of mist in the air like rocket exhaust. They hit the front of the RCG hard enough to send Doug spinning backward. Jarli flinched as the magnetic laser beam swept over him—but it was painless. He had no metal in his body. The magnets didn't affect him.

"Ha!" Doug yelled.

But before he could turn the RCG off, the keys started to crumple against the RCG. The magnetism was stronger than the steel.

"Turn it off!" Jarli cried.

Doug stabbed at the controls. The lamps suspended from the ceiling swung toward the RCG, spotlighting him. One of the chains snapped and a lamp hurtled straight at Doug. He dived out of the way, and the lamp slammed into the RCG. Smashed glass fell through the holes in the catwalk and rained down into the lake of nitrogen. The humming of the machine became a whine, then a scream.

The drones moved toward Doug, but slowly. They were trying to stick to their patrol routes, but the magnet was pulling them backward. They looked like seagulls trapped in the wind.

The catwalk groaned. The magnet was warping the safety rails. Jarli was horrified to see the poles connecting the catwalk to the ceiling were starting to bend toward the RCG.

"Turn it off!" Jarli yelled again.

Doug was still fumbling with the buttons. "I'm trying!"

Finally, the lights on the RCG died and the humming stopped. Instantly, the remaining lamps swung away, released from the magnetic force. The drones shot outward, almost colliding with the distant walls.

Jarli took a deep, shaky breath. "That was close. Let's get—"

One of the poles holding up the catwalk snapped.

Jarli screamed as the catwalk lurched sideways. He hit the safety rail and held on tight.

With a shriek of twisting steel, the other pole broke under the extra weight. One end of the catwalk stayed up, attached to the corridor that led back to the front door. But the other end fell and crashed into the liquid nitrogen. Now the whole catwalk had a steep slope, like a waterslide, leading down into the deadly lake.

Jarli scrabbled wildly against the freezing metal as he slid down the catwalk. Doug managed to grab the safety rail. Jarli didn't. He skidded faster and faster toward the nitrogen pool. He was almost there when he managed to gouge his fingers through the holes in the metal floor of the catwalk. He stopped so suddenly that something popped inside his shoulder.

The lethal mist swirled around him, displacing oxygen. Jarli tried to climb back up, but he was too cold to move. His fingers were clumsy and frozen. He was already dizzy.

Just hold on, he told himself. If he lost his grip, he would slide into the nitrogen pool and freeze to death in seconds.

A bulky figure appeared in the doorway at the top of the sloped catwalk. Through blurring eyes, Jarli recognized him. It was Scanner. He was still in the hazmat suit, but he'd taken his helmet off. He was cradling some kind of tube, like a bazooka.

Scanner looked at Doug, clinging to the safety rail, and then at Jarli, dangling a couple of meters below.

Help us, Jarli said. Or maybe he just thought it. The world was spinning and already seemed strange and dreamlike.

Scanner pointed the bazooka at Doug. With a huge *pop*, a claw shot out, trailing a long cable. The claw snagged Doug's sweater and snapped shut.

Scanner put his tube on the floor and then fixed it in place somehow. The rope started to retract, dragging Doug up the catwalk toward the tube.

After that, Jarli was too dizzy to watch. He rested his head on the cold metal. He couldn't feel his hands anymore.

Then he realized he was falling. His numb hands must have let go.

The mist got thicker and thicker, swallowing him up . . .

And he splashed into the liquid nitrogen.

Frozen Solid

It was like plunging into an ice bath. Worse, even. It was like he'd been teleported into a glacier.

And yet he was dry. Nothing touched his flesh. He was mummified in a protective layer of gas. The Leidenfrost effect—he remembered the name now. But the vapor was melting away, letting the deadly fluid closer and closer to his skin.

He opened his mouth to scream for help—

Then something grabbed his arm. Not a hand. A metal claw.

The claw dragged Jarli out of the pool just as the liquid nitrogen reached his skin. The sudden burn was like an electric shock all over his body. His arms and legs thrashed as the claw dragged him up the catwalk.

"Keep still!" a deep voice yelled. But Jarli had no control over his quaking body. It was as if his arms and legs had been transformed into angry snakes.

As he reached the top of the catwalk, rough hands grabbed him and hauled him through the doorway into the corridor. He found himself looking up at Doug and Scanner.

"Get those shoes and socks off him," Scanner told Doug. "His pants, too. But don't touch them with your bare hands. They're soaked with liquid nitrogen."

Jarli could tilt his head just enough to see the white mist spiraling out of his shoes. A long-lost memory hit him— Kirstie, drawing a picture of him and sticking it to the fridge. Mum, laughing because Kirstie had drawn wavy stink lines coming out of his shoes. He tried to get back to the present, but the present didn't seem real enough to stay in. Maybe this was what dying felt like.

Scanner ripped Jarli's shirt open. Parts of the fabric had frozen and stuck to his skin. It felt like a thousand Band-Aids getting pulled off at once. But Jarli still couldn't breathe well enough to scream.

Scanner put a blanket over Jarli. It was rough, stiff, and heavy. A fire blanket.

"Keep him warm," he said. "The police will be here any minute. When they arrive, it's important that you don't tell them about me."

The sleeves of Doug's jumper were wrapped around his hands. He wrestled Jarli's left shoe off. "Why?"

"I've been undercover in Viper's organization for months," Scanner said. "He sent me and another one of his men to plant a bomb here. I ditched the other guy and came back to disarm it."

"We took care of it," Doug said.

"I know. Using the liquid nitrogen was smart. But if you tell the cops I helped you, Viper will find out. Then he'll kill me."

He showed Doug a scar on the back of his hand, between his thumb and forefinger. "He had me chipped," he said. "Like an animal. There's an RFID sensor under my skin with a capsule of snake venom attached. Viper can murder me with the touch of a button. That's how he keeps his people loyal."

"Those soldiers we saw outside. Do they work for him?"

"No. They're Federal Police. They've locked down the whole town, looking for Viper."

Jarli still couldn't speak. But, as his brain warmed up, he remembered seeing the two hazmat-suited men searching the plane. Scanner had tripped Bagger and taken his time escaping from the garbage bag Bess trapped him in. Could those mistakes have been deliberate? Had he wanted Jarli and Bess to get away?

Doug sounded angry. "If you're a cop, and you're in Viper's organization, why don't you just arrest him?"

"I don't know who he is. No one does. I saw a picture of him once—a man with burns all over his face—but that's not enough for a positive ID. The plane crash was supposed to expose him, but we're not there yet."

"Supposed to?" Doug said. "*You* crashed the plane?"

"Of course not," Scanner said, but something beeped in his pocket. *Lie.*

"Why did I switch that back on?" he grumbled. "That

damn app. You know how hard undercover work is, thanks to you kids?"

"You crashed a plane into my house?" Doug's lip trembled with fury.

"No. Viper did that."

"But you arranged it. Steven Fussell's completely made-up, isn't he? You let Viper *think* there would be someone on that plane who could identify him. Then you planned a flight path right over my house. You *wanted* him to try to crash it. You were hoping to catch him in the act."

"I don't have time to discuss this, and it's classified in any case."

"You could have warned my family."

"They weren't home," Scanner said. "Ask yourself if that was a coincidence."

Had Scanner arranged for Doug's mum to be kept late at work? Jarli spoke through chattering teeth: "You didn't warn the pilot."

"You're awake," Scanner said. "That's my cue to leave. Remember, don't tell anyone I was here. That will blow my cover, and lives will be lost. Definitely mine, and possibly yours."

He stood and walked away up the corridor. Jarli could hear sirens—or maybe his ears were just ringing.

"We have to go," he said. His voice was as rough as a cat's tongue.

"Can you move?" Doug asked.

Jarli tried to sit up, but it was as though his chest weighed a ton. "No."

"Then we'll stay. Here." Doug took off his sweater and helped Jarli put it on. Then he wrapped the fire blanket more tightly around Jarli.

"The cops are coming," Jarli said. "They'll find you."

"Don't worry about that." Doug sounded beaten. "How are you feeling?"

"Not great." Jarli shouldn't have tried to get up. He was dizzy again. It felt like the shivers had spread from his hands and feet to his brain.

"I'm sorry I dragged you into this," Doug said. "And I'm sorry I was always so mean to you."

"It's okay," Jarli croaked. Doug had only been worried about his own family's safety.

"It's not okay. You're a good guy, Jarli. Please don't die."

Jarli tried to stay awake. To reassure Doug that he was going to be fine. But the pain was too much, and he blacked out.

"Liquid nitrogen," Dr. Vorham marveled. "How many seconds would you say you were under?"

"I don't know," Jarli said, squinting against the bright light. "Maybe two?"

Vorham pocketed his miniature flashlight. He was a tall, silver-haired man in his fifties, but his face was strangely wrinkle-free. "Frostbite usually affects the hands and face," he said, "because those areas aren't protected by your clothes. But you have the exact opposite condition, because your clothes soaked up the nitrogen while the Leidenfrost effect shielded your face and hands. There's never been a case quite like this. I could write a paper on you."

"Please don't," Jarli's mum said. She had been there when Jarli woke up, sitting next to his hospital bed, crushing a plastic water bottle with anxious hands. "Will Jarli be okay?"

"Fine, I think," Vorham said. "But you'll have to change his bandages every day until his skin stops peeling off."

That didn't sound "fine" to Jarli. But at least he wasn't going to die.

"Downstairs they'll give you an antiseptic cream to apply with each bandage change," Vorham continued. "Any questions?"

"No," Mum said. "Thank you, Doctor."

With a brisk nod, Dr. Vorham left.

"You're lucky you still have all your fingers and toes," Mum told Jarli. "And *I'm* lucky to be alive—you nearly gave me a heart attack."

"Sorry," Jarli said. He had the feeling he'd be saying that a lot. He cleared his throat. "What time is it?"

Mum checked her watch. "Just after ten."

"Is that a.m. or p.m.?" The ward had no windows, and Jarli had no idea how long he'd been unconscious.

"Ten p.m. You want something to eat?"

"No, thanks. When you called yesterday, those guys who came to our house—who were they? What happened?"

"That was this afternoon," Mum said, "and they were the police. One of them had seen you at the site of the plane crash at night, when you were supposed to be at Bess's house."

She raised her eyebrows at Jarli. Kirstie called this expression Eyebrows of Doom.

"Why didn't you tell me the truth?" Mum asked.

Jarli looked down at his bandages. "I didn't want to worry you."

"Of course," Mum said, gesturing at the hospital ward. "Because all this doesn't worry me at all."

"It's not like I fell into liquid nitrogen on purpose," Jarli said. "It was an accident."

"The police said they went to visit you at school, but you left the school grounds to avoid them. Was that an accident too?"

"I thought they worked for Viper."

Mum's gaze softened. She knew how scared Jarli had been since Viper tried to kill Dad.

"Please, *please* just try to stay safe," she said. "Your father and I have been worried sick."

Staying safe would have meant not helping Bess look for the bolt, and leaving Doug in that underpass to sort out his own problems.

"You have to tell us where you are and what you're doing," Mum added. "Is that so much to ask?"

Jarli changed the subject. "The police at the house—did you get their names?"

"No. There was just one man. Curly hair. Dark around the eyes, like a panda. He asked me to call you. Then he hung up on you when you started talking about Viper."

Jarli wondered why Scanner had done that. Maybe he had thought Jarli was about to blow his cover, and he hadn't wanted to involve Mum.

"Then he left, right?"

Mum nodded. "Pretty much straightaway."

Because Viper had ordered him to plant a bomb. Even after Scanner had rescued him from the liquid nitrogen, Jarli still wondered if he was one of the good guys.

"I'm sorry, Mum," Jarli said. "I was just trying to do the right thing."

"Well, I'm glad you're okay," Mum said, still in her almost-angry voice. "Speaking of police, there are two outside. They arrived when you were unconscious. But you don't have to talk to them if you're not up to it."

"Have they talked to Ter—I mean, to Doug?" Jarli asked.

Mum hesitated.

"What?" Jarli said. "Is Doug okay?"

"We don't know," Mum said. "He's missing."

Good Cop, Bad Cop

S o you can't think of anywhere Doug might have gone?"
Constable Blanco asked.

Jarli shook his head. It was like he'd traveled back in
time. Again, the police wanted to know where Doug was, and
again, he had no idea.

"Answer out loud, please," Blanco said.

She and Frink were sitting by Jarli's hospital bed, phones
out. Using *Truth Premium*, hoping to catch him in a lie. Their
uniforms were impeccable, and neither of them looked tired,
even though they had been chasing bad guys through the
bush late last night. It was like they didn't need sleep. Maybe
they were robots.

Had the bush been last night or the night before? Jarli was
struggling to keep track.

"I don't know where Doug might be," he said. "I thought
he was going to stay in the factory and wait for you guys."

The phones didn't beep. The police looked disappointed.

"Well, he didn't," Frink said. "I found you unconscious in
an empty corridor."

"And after Constable Frink brought you out," Blanco added, "I searched the whole factory, top to bottom. Then the Federal Police turned up, and they searched it too. Doug wasn't there."

Jarli guessed that Doug must have fled, just like after the plane crash. Maybe he thought he would be charged with breaking and entering. But where could he have run to? Back to the underpass?

"You want to talk about what you were doing there?" Frink asked.

"No," Jarli said.

"We also found a bomb," Blanco added. "Big enough to destroy a city block. You want to talk about that?"

"I found it," Jarli said, "and dropped it into some liquid nitrogen to stop it from going off."

"How did you know that would work?"

"I didn't. But it works in video games."

No beeps from the phones, which seemed to shock both cops.

"You're lucky to be alive," Blanco said.

"So I've heard," Jarli said.

"We also found a whole heap of very dangerous tech," Frink put in. "Devices that could be used to bring down a plane."

"Nothing to do with me," Jarli said.

"One of them was missing," Blanco said.

Jarli hesitated. "What do you mean?"

"I pulled the factory inventory," Blanco said. "There were eighteen devices at various stages of completion when the factory closed that day. We only found seventeen."

"Yeah, one was destroyed at the crash site," Jarli said.

"No," Blanco said. "That device was recorded as part of a previous sale. We're talking about a brand-new one, stolen today. It's possible that whoever planted the bomb was trying to hide the theft."

"And the only person we're sure was there," Frink added, "is you."

"Right," Jarli said slowly. "Let me make sure I understand. You think I broke into the Magnotech factory to steal a laser weapon. Then I planted a bomb, hoping to destroy the factory so no one would know the weapon was missing. Then I defused the bomb for some reason?"

"Maybe because you were trapped in the building," Frink put in.

"Uh-huh. Then I dunked myself in liquid nitrogen and blacked out."

"We have no proof that you were genuinely unconscious."

"If I couldn't get out of the building," Jarli asked, "why is the device missing? Where did I hide it?"

Blanco and Frink looked at each other.

"You're a famous programmer," Frink said finally. "Maybe you reprogrammed one of the security drones to take it away."

Jarli laughed. "That's awesome. You should be writing movies. Okay, so how did I make the bomb?"

"Your search history will tell us that," Blanco said. "If you knew how to defuse it, knowing how to make it isn't much of a leap."

"Right. And why did I even want this magnetic weapon in the first place?"

"It's worth a lot of money," Frink said. "To the right buyer."

"Well, let me put your mind at ease," Jarli said. "Make sure your phones are on: I didn't do any of that."

Neither of the phones beeped.

"You programmed the app," Blanco said.

"Not the version you're using."

Blanco ignored this. "You could have made your own voice immune somehow."

"That seems a bit far-fetched," Frink muttered, but Blanco silenced him with a glare.

This made Jarli realize what was going on. They didn't really think he was guilty. They just wanted him to believe they did so he would spill the beans about what really happened.

"Okay, fine," he said. "Here's the truth."

He told them almost everything—that he and Doug had broken into the factory looking for evidence against Viper, that they had found the bomb on their way out, and that they had used one of the magnetic weapons to recover the keys.

If this information somehow found its way to Viper, no harm done—Viper knew it already.

But he left out the return of Scanner. Hopefully that was the right decision. Fortunately, neither of the two police seemed to suspect that anyone else had been involved.

"Did you get the evidence you came for?" Frink asked.

Jarli replied carefully. "I assume it was on the computer in the control room. But there were way too many video files to watch, and I didn't have a flash drive big enough to download them all."

"Did you download any of them?"

"No." True—Jarli had only uploaded. "But you guys can get the videos off the computer, right?"

"Maybe," Blanco said. "Our tech people have had a look at it. Apparently, some kind of virus deleted everything."

Whoops. Jarli swallowed. That wasn't what the virus he'd installed was supposed to do. Had there been a bug in the code?

"But just because it was deleted doesn't mean it's gone forever," Blanco continued. "Our team is working on it."

She didn't mention the burner phone Jarli had plugged in. Maybe she didn't realize it was his, and didn't want him to know they'd found it. "Are you going to arrest me for breaking into Magnotech?" Jarli asked, trying not to sound scared.

"What do you think, Constable Frink?" Blanco asked.

"I think the department's priorities lie elsewhere, Constable Blanco," Frink said.

Dangerous Knowledge

For two days, nothing much happened.

Kirstie posted a theory on social media that Jarli had been abducted by aliens, and that his sudden frostbite could only have come from exposure to the vacuum of space. She got some enthusiastic comments from some very sketchy people, and then Mum and Dad made her delete the post.

The lockdown was lifted and the Federal Police left. Jarli guessed that they had given up the search, for now. Viper's trail had gone cold.

Bess came back from Warbydale farm. No point hiding anymore, since the people looking for her had turned out to be the good guys. She said she'd had a good time, and was now thinking of buying a farm when she grew up. Apparently, she'd befriended a cow.

Jarli went back to school. The burns itched, and he had to move carefully to avoid tearing the new skin. He was excused from PE, but not his other classes. The bandages and Kirstie's outrageous rumours about his absence made him a home-room celebrity for about two hours. Then two popular kids,

Tammy and Sam, broke up. After that, everyone forgot all about him.

Hiding had been scary, but not-hiding was even worse. Jarli kept looking over his shoulder, wondering if Viper would send someone to attack him. But the police had told him that there was nothing to worry about. He didn't know enough to be a target.

Doug was still missing. Jarli and Bess had checked the underpass, the storage unit, and the ruins of his house. No sign of him.

Now Jarli was in his bedroom, staying clear of Mum and Dad. Their anger had bubbled away, leaving only worry, which was almost worse. They had become completely overprotective, fussing over his burns and watching him like eagles.

Jarli stared at the security video on his computer screen. Even at 4X speed, it was so boring he thought it might be giving him brain damage. Strangers entered Magnotech's foyer and left again. Cars pulled in and out of the parking lot. There was no sound, and the footage was just blurry enough to hurt his eyes.

Jarli still couldn't figure out why the virus had deleted everything on the control room computer. That shouldn't have happened. But his plan had worked. The virus had transmitted hundreds of hours of footage to the server in India. Hacking it was easier than Jarli had expected. It used a proxy server, but Jarli could break through by overloading the proxy with requests from a shell script. And they had a tough firewall, but the OUROBOROS virus was permitted to bypass it in order to deliver stolen files to them.

So Jarli had modified the virus. He'd changed the destination IP address so the files would be sent to his computer, rather than to India. Then he'd sent the virus back to them. The Indian hacker had been burgled by his own virus.

Jarli was thrilled with his own cleverness, but he couldn't tell anyone about it. What he had done was probably illegal.

The only problem was that Jarli's hard drive had quickly filled up with millions of other people's stolen files. It had taken him a while to work out how to automatically delete everything that wasn't a security video from Magnotech.

A knock at his door.

"Jarli," Mum said. "We're going out to buy Kirstie some new shoes. You want to come?"

"No, thanks," Jarli said, without looking away from the screen.

"Okay. Well, don't go anywhere until we come back." Mum's footsteps padded away.

After he heard the front door close, Jarli wondered if the invitation had been an olive branch. Maybe his mother was trying to say Jarli had been forgiven for lying and putting himself in danger. But it was too late now, and he had hours of lethally boring videos to watch.

Jarli couldn't give up. Doug wouldn't come out of hiding

until Viper had been identified. And Dana Reynolds said she'd run out of leads. Jarli had sent her the videos, but he didn't hold out much hope.

The problem was that they didn't know what they were looking for. Jarli had hoped to spot a man with burns on his face, or a snake tattoo or something. But the resolution was too low. Any of the people walking in and out of Magnotech could have been Viper. And Doug's parents were still missing. Without Doug's mother to provide the exact date when the RCG device was meant to get picked up, Jarli was at a dead end.

The doorbell rang.

His family must have forgotten something. It was like the universe was giving him another chance to go with them.

He paused the video and switched off the screen so they wouldn't see what he had been doing. Then he limped over to answer the door, trying not to aggravate his burns.

It wasn't Mum and Dad, which made sense. They wouldn't ring their own doorbell. It was Constable Frink, with a sports bag under one arm and a bundle of folders under the other. No sign of a car, or of Blanco.

"Jarli," he said. "Are your mum and dad home?"

"You just missed them," Jarli said. "What do you want?"

"I know who Viper is," Frink said. He patted the folders. "I've brought some photos."

This announcement was so astounding that Jarli half

expected his phone to beep. But it didn't. Frink was telling the truth.

"Can I come in?" Frink asked.

Jarli nodded and stood aside.

Frink entered the house, looking around at the framed family photos and open doorways. He seemed anxious. "Viper's identity is a dangerous thing to know," he said, placing the manila folders on the dinner table. "I have to ask—are you sure you want to be part of this?"

"Yes," Jarli said. He wasn't going to give up now. And it wasn't like *not* knowing had kept him safe.

"Is there anyone else in the house?" Frink asked. "Can anyone hear us?"

"No."

"All right." Frink gestured to the folders and stepped back. "Take a look."

Jarli sat down at the table. He opened the first folder and found a bundle of photos, printed on cheap paper. They showed several people of various ages and ethnicities, engaged in various activities. None of the pictures were labeled.

"Which one is . . ." Jarli began. Then there was a sharp pain at the back of his neck, like a bee sting.

"Ow!" he said. He twisted his head to see what had hurt him.

Frink was holding a syringe.

"What . . ." Jarli began. "I don't . . ."

Frink put a cap on the syringe and pocketed it. Then he stood back, glancing at his watch.

Jarli tried to stand up, but he couldn't. Something cold was spreading out from his neck across his shoulders and down his spine. He couldn't move his arms or legs. It felt as though he was turning to stone.

"Don't fight it," Frink said. "That never works."

Jarli tried to swing a fist at Frink, but he couldn't even close his hand. His vision blurred.

The last thing he saw before he blacked out was Frink laying a huge sheet of plastic on the floor.

Prisoner Transport

Jarli dreamed he was in the cockpit of a plane. There was no pilot. Through the windscreen, he could see the ground. The plane was falling out of the sky. He could feel it getting faster and faster. His organs were swimming around in his chest. Below was Doug's house, getting bigger and bigger . . .

"Argh!" Jarli woke to find himself in pitch blackness. He was tangled up in a blanket—no, a plastic sheet. It covered his whole body, including his face. It had been tied around him with nylon ropes. There was a rumbling sound in the air, and the floor was vibrating beneath him.

Ignoring the pain from his burns, Jarli writhed like a caterpillar in a cocoon. The ropes weren't tight enough to hold him now that he was conscious. He pulled them down over his hips and wriggled out of the sheet, heart pounding.

Then he remembered: Frink.

Jarli was in a vehicle; that much was clear. A van. Maybe the same one he had seen at the crash site.

One of the two hazmat guys, Scanner, had been the man

with the dark circles around his eyes. Could the other one, Bagger, have been Frink? Yes—he was about the right size, and had the same color hair.

Jarli crawled around the back of the van, eyes wide in the dark. His legs were too wobbly to stand up, and he couldn't see a single speck of light. A frightening thought struck him. What if it wasn't dark? What if the stuff Frink had used to knock him out had blinded him?

Jarli checked his pockets for his phone. He had retrieved it from the alley yesterday, but now it was gone again.

If Frink was Viper, that explained how Cobra, Viper's assassin, had vanished from his police cell. It also revealed how Viper always seemed to be one step ahead of the investigation. It even explained why Priya had vanished. Doug thought she had gone to look for the police. Maybe Frink was the first police officer she had found.

Then what had he done with her? And with Doug's parents? A cold feeling spread through Jarli's belly.

Blanco's voice echoed through his mind. *After Constable Frink brought you out, I searched the whole factory, top to bottom. Then the Federal Police turned up, and they searched it too. Doug wasn't there.*

Doug hadn't fled. Frink had already caught him. Maybe he'd thrown Doug into the liquid nitrogen, or sealed him in one of the crates in the garage.

For a moment, Jarli's terror was washed away by grief.

Doug, the friendless boy who just wanted to make robots, had left his whole world behind. He had spent a year pretending to be someone else, trusting no one. And that still hadn't been enough to save him from Viper.

Wherever Frink was taking him, Jarli didn't want to go there. Viper was willing to kill people who knew too much. That included Jarli now. Blind or not, he had to get out of this van before it reached its destination.

He crawled over to what felt like the back door, and fumbled around until he felt the handle. Then he hesitated. The engine was still rumbling, the floor still shaking. The van felt like it was going fast. If Jarli jumped out, the gravel would rip his bandages to shreds and destroy the tender new skin underneath.

He grabbed the plastic sheeting and wrapped it tightly around himself. It wouldn't provide much cushioning when he hit the road. But it might just stop him from losing too much skin to run away.

A factoid from history class surfaced in his mind: When the nuclear bomb destroyed Nagasaki, some people had survived just because an extra shirt protected them from the radiation.

Jarli took a deep breath and reached for the handle.

Then the van started to slow down. It had arrived. He was too late.

Jarli twisted the handle anyway.

The door didn't open. Locked from outside.

Brakes squeaking, the van stopped. Jarli lay back down in the blackness, still half-wrapped in the plastic. He found one end of the nylon rope, held it, and rolled over, winding it around himself. Maybe he could convince Frink he was still unconscious.

Footsteps crunched around the van. Jarli mummified himself in plastic and lay still just as the back door opened.

Even through closed eyelids and the plastic sheeting, Jarli saw the daylight flood into the van. He wasn't blind! He had to stop himself from crying out with relief.

Someone grabbed the plastic and pulled it. Jarli was dragged feetfirst toward the open door. His legs were out in the open air before he realized the person pulling wasn't going to stop.

THUMP! Jarli fell out of the van and hit the dirt, burned skin smarting. He was unable to suppress a grunt.

"Yeah, I thought you'd be awake by now." Frink's voice. "Get up."

Jarli emerged from the cocoon of plastic and looked around. He was at the quarry on the outskirts of Kelton. He and Kirstie used to come here on their bikes, riding dangerously close to the cliff edge. Frink's van was the only vehicle in sight, all the way to the horizon. Everything valuable had been ripped out of the ground long ago. Frink had the place to himself.

A shipping container stood nearby. Windows had been

cut into the sides, and an air-conditioning unit installed on top. Maybe it had been used as the site office, back when the quarry was still active. But now there were bars on the windows, and the glass had been painted black. Jarli could hear muffled screams from inside the container. "Help us! Somebody! Please! *Help!*"

"Three days now, they've been doing that," Frink said. "It hasn't done them any good. We're a long way from anywhere. No one's coming. You got that?"

He was holding a handgun. Jarli didn't know much about guns, but it looked like the kind that probably had at least six bullets in it. And Frink was a police officer—he would have good aim.

Jarli was shaking. He could hardly breathe. "Why are you doing this?"

"I'll ask the questions," Frink said. "And this time I want the truth."

"I told you everything already," Jarli said.

Frink's phone beeped. *Lie.* He smiled. "That's what I thought." He tossed Jarli a ring of keys. "Open that container."

Jarli went over to the shipping container. Opening the doors would be complicated. There were four handles, each padlocked, all attached to vertical bars. As soon as he started fiddling, the screaming intensified. The people inside thought they were getting rescued.

The key ring had four large keys and one smaller one. The

four big keys matched the padlocks. Jarli guessed that the small one was a handcuff key. As he worked on the padlocks, Jarli slipped the small key off the ring and hid it in the palm of his hand. If Frink cuffed him, he could use the key to get away—assuming Frink didn't notice it was missing.

"Hurry up," Frink said.

"I'm trying."

Finally, the doors creaked open. A foul smell washed out. Light fell across the faces of the four people inside.

Doug.

Priya, the pilot.

Two middle-aged blond people who were probably Doug's parents. Missing for three days now. When their home was destroyed, Frink must have sent them a message, telling them to meet him somewhere safe. Safe for him.

"Oh, thank God," Priya said when she saw Jarli. Then she saw Frink standing behind him and her face collapsed.

The back half of the shipping container was filled with transparent plastic crates of clothes and documents. One huge crate contained nothing but fifty-dollar notes. Jarli had never seen so much money in one place.

The missing RCG device sat on top of one of the crates, out of reach of the captives. Blanco must have been right about the reason for the bomb. Viper had wanted the police to think all the magnetic weapons had been destroyed.

The front half of the container was being used as a prison.

There were a single water bottle and a bucket, which Jarli guessed was used as a toilet. All four prisoners were chained to the walls by their ankles, which explained why Frink had been happy to leave them alone with his crate of money. They wouldn't be able to reach it.

The sadness in their eyes was horrible. Doug's parents looked gaunt and frail in the glare of the sun. Priya had survived a plane crash and turned to the police, only to discover that she had trusted the wrong cop.

Doug's face was grim, but he didn't look as ruined as the others. He hadn't been a prisoner for as long. He still had hope.

Jarli's back was turned to Frink. He met Doug's gaze and flashed the handcuff key in his hand.

"Throw the keys back to me," Frink said.

Jarli had never been good at sports, and he had never expected his life to depend on a perfect throw.

He took a deep breath and turned around. He tossed the key ring over to Frink. He deliberately threw it too high. While Frink was looking up, Jarli concealed his other hand behind his back and flicked the handcuff key backward, hoping Doug would catch it.

He didn't hear it hit the floor of the shipping container. With any luck, that meant someone had caught it. But it wasn't as though he had given them much of an advantage. They were weak, and Frink was armed.

Frink caught the ring of keys.

"What are you going to do to us?" Jarli asked, distracting Frink so he didn't notice that the handcuff key had been removed from his key ring.

"That depends," Frink said, "on whether or not you tell the truth."

Jarli said nothing.

"Every time you lie to me," Frink continued, "I'm going to shoot one of your friends." He held up his phone. "And believe me, I'll know."

Jarli could feel his heart racing faster and faster. He tried to take deep breaths—the app looked for signs of nervousness.

"Question one," Frink said. "Do you know who Viper is?"

Final Round

sn't it you?" Jarli asked.

"I'm not Viper," Frink said.

His phone didn't beep.

"Now you know that," Frink said, "do you have any suspects?"

"No." Jarli racked his brain for something he could say to stall Frink. Then he remembered a clue: "He's a man with scars on his face."

"You've seen the picture."

Jarli nodded vigorously. If he admitted he hadn't seen it, Frink would ask who told Jarli about it. That might put Eaton or Scanner in danger.

Frink had said "the picture," not "a picture." Was there only one? Had Frink only seen his sinister boss in a photograph?

Frink didn't seem to notice that Jarli hadn't answered out loud. "Question two," he said. "What do you know about Viper's operation?"

Jarli kept his eyes on the phone. He couldn't lie. "Only know what Blanco told me, months ago."

"Which was what?"

"He makes people disappear. I don't know how."

The phone didn't beep.

"Question three," Frink said.

Cold sweat ran into Jarli's eyes. If Frink asked about Scanner, Jarli would be forced to tell the truth. But if he did, Viper would know he had a leak in his organization. *Lives will be lost. Definitely mine, and possibly yours.*

But that wasn't what Frink asked.

"What evidence," he said, "did you extract from the computer in the control room at Magnotech?"

"Videos of people going in and out of the building," Jarli said.

"How did you get them off the computer?"

"I used a computer virus."

"That was your phone I found plugged into the computer?"

"No," Jarli said. "It was Doug's."

This explained why Blanco hadn't asked about the burner phone. Frink had removed it before she got there. He must have also deleted all the files on the computer. The virus hadn't malfunctioned after all.

"Did you send this footage to anyone else?"

Jarli's heart sank. He was going to have to sell Reynolds out.

Frink's eyes narrowed. "Did you send or show this footage to anybody?"

"Yes," Jarli said.

"Who?"

"Dana Reynolds."

"The reporter?"

Jarli nodded.

"When?"

"Yesterday."

Frink pressed a few buttons on his phone and held it to his ear.

"Viper," he said. "We have a problem."

Jarli could faintly hear Viper speaking, but he couldn't make out the words. The voice was distorted with some kind of filter, turning it into a rasping growl. The sound made Jarli's skin crawl.

Once Viper had destroyed all the video evidence, he would order Frink to kill the witnesses—Jarli, Reynolds, and the four people in the shipping container. Jarli had doomed them all.

"No," Frink was saying. "Durras doesn't know anything important. But he has the footage from Magnotech. He sent it to a journalist, Dana Reynolds."

Viper said something else.

"Yesterday," Frink said. "She may already have watched it. If so, she's seen me meeting with the engineer."

The Federal Police had been wrong, Jarli realized. Viper had not collected the RCG in person. The evidence they'd collected could prove Frink was guilty, but wouldn't help them find Viper.

"I need to disappear," Frink said. "Can you book me in?"

Viper said something. Just one syllable.

"Okay," Frink said. "What should I do with the prisoners?"

He listened for a minute.

"All of them?" he said.

Viper said something else.

"Okay," Frink said again.

He turned to the open doorway of the container and aimed his gun at the prisoners. At this range, he couldn't possibly miss.

"No!" Jarli screamed. "Don't!"

Ignoring him, Frink fired directly into the open doorway. Eight deafening shots rang out.

Then he swiveled and pointed the gun at Jarli.

Jarli turned to dive out of the way—

But it was too late. At point-blank range, Frink pulled the trigger three times.

BANG. BANG. BANG.

No Escape

arli slammed into the dirt and rolled sideways. The sun dazzled him.

There was pain. But only from the torn skin under his bandages, and the rocks digging into his shoulder blades.

None of the bullets had hit him.

Frink noticed this. Scowling, he leveled the gun at Jarli again—

And then it flew out of his hand. The gun disappeared into the shipping container, where Doug was holding the RCG. He had freed himself and switched it on.

The gun hit the device and crumpled like paper. A halo of bullets was also stuck to the RCG, quivering. The magnet had sucked them out of the air.

His heart pounding, Jarli saw the other three prisoners cowering on the floor. No one seemed to have been hit by the gunfire.

Frink, now unarmed, looked like he was trying to figure out how Doug had gotten loose.

"What—" he began.

Then Jarli tackled him.

Frink was bigger, but Jarli had the element of surprise. The phone went flying from Frink's hand as he hit the ground. Doug dropped the RCG and scrambled over, grabbing one of Frink's arms while Jarli held the other.

"No!" Frink shouted. "Don't!"

In the shipping container, the fallen RCG was whining louder and louder. Doug hadn't switched it off. The handcuff chains were straining in the air, trying to reach it. The metal walls of the shipping container began to buckle inward. Soon the other prisoners would be crushed.

Jarli was still wrestling with Frink, but he saw that Priya had unlocked her chains. "Priya," he yelled. "Turn off the device!"

Frink ripped his arm out of Doug's grip and tried to punch Jarli. Jarli grabbed his wrist just in time. Doug regained his hold on the loose arm and pushed Frink back down.

Priya grabbed the RCG. "How?"

"Red button," Doug shouted. "On the underside!"

Priya found the button, and the whining stopped. The container stopped creaking and settled on the concrete slab.

"You idiots!" Frink roared. "You don't know what you're doing!"

Priya ran over and grabbed Frink's legs. Together they dragged him toward the shipping container.

Doug fastened some of the cuffs around Frink's ankles, then got to work freeing his parents.

Jarli went to pick up the phone Frink had dropped. A phone number glowed on the screen.

Viper's number. He was still connected.

"Don't touch that!" Frink cried.

Jarli ignored him. He picked up the phone.

"Viper," he said. "This is Jarli Durras. We've captured Frink."

"Shut up!" Frink hissed.

Viper said nothing.

"So there's no point going after Dana Reynolds," Jarli continued. "She might have video files of Frink picking up the RCG from the engineer, but Frink's busted either way. It's over."

The only sound was the faint hiss of static. But Jarli could somehow sense that Viper was listening.

"It's over," Jarli said again. "The prisoners are free. We have Frink, and the RCG, and the money. The cops will find you soon. You should turn yourself in."

Viper was a slippery character, but Jarli didn't see how he could escape now. Frink knew who Viper was. He had said so when he turned up at Jarli's house, and Jarli's phone hadn't beeped.

"Ow," Frink said. "Ow!"

Jarli looked over. Frink was clutching his hand. The one with the scar. Jarli could see a faint glow through his skin. As if something was under there.

The other prisoners backed away from him.

"What *is* that?" Doug's father asked.

Frink didn't reply. His eyes had rolled back into his head. Churned-up spit leaked from the corners of his mouth. His arms and legs quivered, as though he was freezing.

And then, suddenly, he lay still.

"Frink?" Jarli said.

Frink didn't reply. Something he'd said flashed through Jarli's mind: *Viper's identity is a dangerous thing to know.*

Jarli looked back at the phone.

Viper had hung up.

Cleanup Crew

The debriefing officer had black hair, cut army-short. Her dark eyes were watchful, and she spoke in a clipped monotone. She had introduced herself as Detective Zee Arno.

"The pathologist said it was an RFID chip. It was linked to a capsule filled with . . ." She rummaged through some papers, and then gave up. ". . . some kind of poison. I forget which one. Viper activated the chip using Daniel Frink's phone. If you'd been standing a little farther away from him, it wouldn't have worked."

Arno didn't seem to care how Jarli might feel about this. He looked down at his hands. They were still shaking. He'd been through a lot—the plane crash, the tunnels under Kelton, the liquid nitrogen—but he'd never seen someone die before.

Doug's parents had used Frink's phone to call emergency services. By the time the ambulance arrived, Frink's body was already cold. Everyone had been taken to the hospital except Jarli, who had come straight to the police station. He had told Arno the whole story—almost. He hadn't told her about Scanner. And he hadn't told her about the tunnel under the school, because he'd made a promise to Nurse Eaton.

Rule number five: Don't trust anybody.

"You already know what happened, mostly," Arno said. "Viper ordered an RCG device from Magnotech and sent Frink to pick it up. Then Viper used the device to crash a plane into your friend's house, hoping to sabotage a federal investigation. But the device was damaged in the crash and the intended victims survived. So Viper sent Frink to capture the pilot and your friend's family. He also ordered more RCG devices from Magnotech, to replace the broken one."

"Why?" Jarli asked.

"We don't know. But Frink's prisoners overheard other phone calls between him and Viper. It sounded like Viper had at least one other target. Our theory is that Frink planted the bomb so that pieces of the devices would be scattered everywhere. After the explosion, we'd never realize one was missing. Thanks to you and Doug, the factory was not destroyed and we became aware of the theft. The stolen device has since been recovered from the quarry."

"What does the owner of Magnotech know about all this?" Jarli asked. "Kellin Plowman?"

"Possibly nothing," Arno said sharply. "It's an unmanned factory. Other than the engineer who died, we can't be sure that any other employees knew about Viper. I'd advise you to give Plowman a wide berth while we investigate. Understood?"

Jarli nodded. "Is Dana Reynolds okay?"

"Yes. We sent units over to her house and her office. No one was there who shouldn't be, but the protective detail will stay for a while just in case. It's lucky you and Doug got the drop on Frink when you did. If you hadn't, Frink would have killed all the witnesses, delivered the RCG to Viper, and, presumably, come after Reynolds."

So I killed Frink to save Reynolds, Jarli thought. That was definitely better than the other way around, but it still felt wrong. He should have realized Frink would be chipped. He shouldn't have tried to talk to Viper on the phone.

"Is Reynolds still in danger?" he asked.

"I doubt it. Knowing about Frink would have made her a target, but now the cat's out of the bag."

"How's Constable Blanco taking the news?"

"She's suspended while internal affairs investigates."

Jarli's eyes widened. "You think she was involved?"

"It doesn't look good," Arno said. "Her partner was corrupt. That makes her either complicit or oblivious. Neither is acceptable."

"Can you trace the call from Frink's phone?" Jarli said. "To find Viper?"

Arno shook her head. "The number Frink dialed led us to a burner phone in an abandoned warehouse. No calls were ever made by it. It was only used to receive calls from Frink."

"Can you figure out where it was sold, maybe?"

"We already did. It was purchased with cash from a gas station here in Kelton. We pulled the surveillance videos from the day in question. Frink bought it himself." She pressed her pen against a sheet of paper, as though hoping to bore a hole through it. "Viper's smart, and smart criminals avoid touching evidence themselves. Even if we knew who Viper was, we might struggle to prosecute him."

"So what about Doug?" Jarli asked.

"He's going to a motel with his parents while we look for a new house for them."

Jarli wondered what Doug's name would be next time. "Will I get to say good-bye?"

"You don't have to. They're staying in Kelton."

"Really? Viper tried to kill him and his whole family—"

"To stop his mother from meeting with Steven Fussell. The two of them might have seen Frink on the security video from the factory and realized he was working for Viper. But there's no point protecting Frink anymore. And, according to the Federal Police, there was never any such person as Steven Fussell. It was a trick, designed to lure Viper into the open. Viper has probably figured that out by now."

"How can Doug's family be sure they're safe here, though?"

"We offered them new identities." Arno leaned forward, threading her fingers together. "But they refused to take them. Doug's parents don't trust the police anymore. I suppose I don't blame them. It was Frink who organized their last move, so Viper probably knew where they were going before they did. Anyway, they said they were sick of running. And Doug said he didn't want to leave his friends."

Epilogue

Y ou forgot one thing," Snake Man told the alien queen. "I
can *shed my skin*."

"Noooo!" the alien shrieked.

Bess threw some popcorn at the screen. "This is dumb."

"It might be the silliest movie that has ever existed," Doug
agreed, resting his feet on the coffee table.

"Hey, I was happy to watch it alone," Jarli said. He hated it
when people made fun of movies he liked. "You two insisted
on coming over."

"Only because a plane crash stopped me from watching it the
first time," Bess said. "It would feel like defeat to *not* be here."

"So you're not enjoying it, you're just stubborn."

"Determined," Bess corrected.

"And you definitely weren't crying when Snake Man's
sister—"

"No," Bess snapped. "I just needed to blow my nose."

Jarli's phone buzzed.

"You said you wouldn't use your app on me," Bess com-
plained.

"That wasn't my app." Jarli picked up the phone. It was a message from an unknown sender.

Come outside

Spiders of fear danced on Jarli's spine. He showed the message to Bess.

Her eyes widened. "Could be just someone messing with you . . ." Jarli had received death threats and other sinister communications when his app first went viral.

"Could be," he agreed.

"I think this movie might actually be worse than the plane crash that destroyed my house," Doug said, oblivious.

"Shut up. Look at this." Jarli showed him the message. His phone buzzed again as a second text came in.

You know how hard undercover work is, thanks to you?

"Scanner," Jarli and Doug said at the same moment.

"Who?" Bess asked.

"Give me a second." Jarli went to the front door and opened it. No one was there, but an unfamiliar car was parked on the other side of the street. A black sedan, recently washed.

The headlights flashed twice, signaling Jarli.

Jarli walked over. The window rolled down. The driver was Scanner.

"Get in," he said.

Jarli hopped into the passenger side. The car smelled like it had been washed recently. The leather was soft and warm. Jarli thought there might be an automatic seat warmer in it. Maybe this was Viper's car.

Scanner didn't wait for Jarli to put his seat belt on. He pulled out onto the road and zoomed off.

"Did you tell Detective Arno about me?" Scanner asked.

"No," Jarli said.

"Good. Because this is far from over. We still don't know why Viper wanted a second RCG weapon after he'd already brought down the plane."

"Maybe to sell to a terrorist group?" Jarli couldn't remember who had suggested this, but the idea had stuck in his mind.

"No. If that were the case, Viper wouldn't have tried to blow up the factory to cover up the theft. He would have wanted everyone to know he had an RCG to sell. Instead, he was trying to make it look like they had all been destroyed. Which means he had a second target, and we don't know who. That makes me nervous. I don't like not knowing things."

"Where are we going?" Jarli asked.

"Just around the block," Scanner said. "This car is LoJacked. If I stop in one place for too long, it sends a notification to Viper. There was an audio bug too, but I disabled it. He can't hear us."

"Do you know who he is?"

"Not yet." Scanner reached the end of the street and turned the corner. "I've identified several other people who work for him, but most of them haven't met him, and all of them are chipped. They won't help the cops."

"So why are you here?"

"I wanted to tell you that Viper is no longer actively pursuing you, your family, or your friends. As far as he knows, you don't have any important information."

"As far as he knows?"

Scanner turned another corner. "You know about me. He doesn't."

It sounded like a threat.

"I don't know anything about you," Jarli said. "I don't even know your name."

"You know I work for Viper and that I'm actually a cop. That's enough to make you a danger to me."

The car was driving faster and faster. Jarli gripped the sides of his seat.

"You've foiled Viper's plans twice now," Scanner continued, "and met several of his operatives. If he realizes he has a leak in his organization, he might start to wonder if you know who it is. This would leave me in a difficult position."

Jarli thought about Priya—the pilot who had nearly been sacrificed to identify Viper. How many more people was the government willing to kill to expose him?

Scanner swerved, hard. The g-force pushed Jarli toward the passenger door. He suddenly wondered if Scanner was trying to roll the car. He could make it look like Jarli had died in a car accident.

But then Viper would know he had picked Jarli up. And Scanner could just as easily die in the crash.

The car screeched to a stop. Jarli looked out the window and saw his own house. They had gone all the way around the block.

"So stay out of Viper's way," Scanner said. "Forget all about him. And maybe he'll forget about you too."

"Is that a threat?"

"It's advice. Now get out."

Jarli climbed out of the car shakily. It sped off as soon as he closed the door, leaving a haze of exhaust in the air.